EROS

PSYCHE

A RETELLING

BY SOPHIA BLIS

Table of Contents

I The God of Desire 6

II When Aphrodite Demands 10

III Boredom and Apricot Spears 12

IV Evil Spirits and Dropped Arrows 14

V A Test Unpassed 18

VI Thank Gods for No Suitors? 20

VII Anteros Gives Advice and Eros Listens 23

VIII Oracle Speaks of Monsters 26

IX Building Mortal Palaces 28

X Winds of Change 30

XI A Hurricane with Edges 34

XII Flying Through Twilight 37

XIII When the God of War Calls 41

XIV There Be Monsters There 44

XV Upwards 47

XVI A Monster with Wings 48

XVII Disappear Into Forever 54

XVIII Oil Lamps and the End of the World 58

XIX Agonizing Betrayal 64

XX Anteros, a Crowd of Cupids, and a Question 65

XXI Two Sides of a Coin 67

XXII Abandoned by the Gods 70

XXIII A Favor Returned 74
XXIV The Begetting of the Tasks..................................76
XXV The Seeds 78
XXVI A Lucid Moment 82
XXVII Where Do the Forsaken Go? 83
XXVIII Third Task...87
XXIX Crossing a River 89
XXX All Roads Lead to Hades......................................92
XXXI Darkness in Light 97
XXXII Light in Darkness 98
XXXIII The Only Right Thing......................................100
ACKNOWLEDGMENTS 104
More Works By Sophia Blis 105

Copyright © 2022 Sophia Blis

All rights reserved. No portion of this book may be reproduced in any form without permission from the publisher, except as permitted by U.S. copyright law.

Cover Illustration © 2022 by Sophia Blis.

To the one

I The God of Desire

Eros was the god of desire and the son of the goddess of love and when he got bored, he liked to play tricks. His arrows were an ideal pastime, for no mortal or god could resist them. At least not when Eros hit them. Over the millennia, most of the gods have developed countless methods of evasion but that amused Eros even more.

"Are you even listening to me?" Zeus said. The King of Gods looked young and handsome wrapped in an ivory toga but still there was an aura of ancientness to him. Not that it stopped the arrows from hitting him. In fact, Zeus was one of the easiest targets.

Eros leaned back into the alcove of clouds. "No."

Zeus gritted his teeth and thunder rumbled in the distance.

"Now, now," Eros said. "There's no harm in repeating."

"For the last time, make Callisto fall in love with me."

"No."

"Why not?"

"That arrow," he waved, and a faint ghost of an arrow appeared in Zeus's ribcage, "was meant for Artemis and you got in the way. Again."

"I was there on official business."

Eros laughed. "Right."

"You're forgetting who you're speaking to."

"And you're developing an addiction problem. Too many of my arrows are not good for you, you know."

"Eros," Zeus let out an indignant breath, "my patience is running thin. You will help me or I will strip you of your godhood."

"Zeus," Eros said, getting mock serious, "you and I both know what would happen if you stripped me of my godhood. No love," he said as a tender cloud heart appeared in one palm, "no children," on the other palm, a fluff of cloud became an infant. "No children," he continued as the child turned into a bowing adult, "no worshippers," both clouds withered away. "And we all know what would become of gods without worship."

"You insolent—"

Just then, a cherub floated in. "Master Eros, there is a girl come to your temple in the earthen plane. She says she wants her heart back."

"Are you new?" Eros asked, considering the intruder. The child was lean and swathed in a snow-white toga and silvery wings. Cherubs came into existence when someone dreamed of love in their sleep. They separated from the dream and found their way to Eros's abode. It used to be irritating to find babies at his doorstep every morning, but they've proved their worth over the years.

"Yes," the cherub replied.

"Hmm, well, see that you don't bother me with such trivial matters again."

"Yes, of course," the cherub said, surprised. "I just thought you'd want to know."

"Well, I don't," Eros said and motioned for him to go.

"You will help me," Zeus said once they were alone again.

Eros sighed. "Now who's not listening? But fine I'll repeat my answer. No."

"Then at least undo this." Zeus pointed to the arrow.

Eros laughed again. "And miss all the fun? Not a chance."

Lightning spidered through the clouds of Eros's abode, turning tender pinks into ashen greys. A deafening roar of thunder echoed through the chambers and one of the cherubs fell through a hole that was created at the end of the hall.

"Watch it," Eros said. "*I don't go around destroying gods' homes.*"

"One day you will know the sting of love and I will laugh at you."

"I'm sure the whole Olympus will," Eros said. "Which is why that day will never come."

Eros's arrows only worked when he shot them, and he wasn't about to go shooting himself.

With a final flare of his nostrils, Zeus disappeared.

Anteros, Eros's brother, flew in through the open hole in the clouds, looking at it questioningly. "What did you do this time?" he asked, settling down on a cumulus.

"Something fun."

"Yes, sure, we all know your definition of fun." Anteros said, summoning a cherub for a glass of ambrosia. "And speaking of not fun things, I heard mother was coming over tonight."

Eros screwed up his lips. "Anything interesting?"

"She's having another crisis."

"What is it this time?"

"A beautiful maiden stealing her worshippers."

"Again?" Eros itched his brow. "Didn't the same thing happen last decade? And the decade before that." There were many humans who were beautiful and lately Aphrodite's been becoming more and more insecure about them. Every time a beautiful girl was born, she'd ask Eros to make her fall in love with a wart ridden brute, knowing full well that his arrows could cause great agony. And every time Anteros would insist that Eros take his arrows instead, so the love between the two would at least be the kind that lasted with the eternal fire of selflessness.

"I think she's in a wrathful mood," Anteros said. "The girl is nothing to be worried about."

"You checked?"

Anteros inclined his head.

"Are you sure that I can't just have a little fun with this one? Maybe I could make her fall in love with her own reflection."

"Remember how well that ended for Narcissus?"

Eros shrugged. "I think he's better off as a flower."

"And Echo."

"Yes, well, I don't think she has it too bad."

Anteros fixed Eros with a grave look. "Mortals already have it rough on earth and this girl will have it worse. Can you imagine being hated by Aphrodite?"

"No."

"Well, I can."

Eros let out an impatient sigh. "Fine, give me your arrows."

Anteros summoned a quiver of arrows between them. Unlike Eros's golden ones, his arrows were made of polished wood and, as contrary as that might seem, built to last.

"While we're at it. Can you go take care of the mortal at my altar in Athens?" Eros asked, taking a few of Anteros's arrows. "Make certain she finds a suitable partner and makes lots of devout children."

Anteros took a sip of ambrosia and stood up. "Of course." And then he was off.

What a boring brother Eros had.

II When Aphrodite Demands

The moment Aphrodite glimmered into the clouds the sun shone brighter.

The Gratiae and Horae, minor gods and goddesses that dogged her every step, strew wreaths and flower petals in front of her. Notos, the god of the south wind gently stirred her garments dyed in flowers of Spring- hyacinths and roses, lilies and narcissuses, crocuses and violets. The gods all waved or winked at Eros as she neared.

Eros smiled. He was always one for theatrics.

"My darling boy," his mother said, hugging Eros as gently as seafoam hugs the shore. She focused all her charms on him and when Aphrodite did that, not even the gods could withstand it.

Eros welcomed her inside, while the cherubs prepared ambrosia and nectar for the Goddess.

"Did you expand your abode?" she asked, frowning at the hole in the cloud floor.

"Courtesy of Zeus."

"What an infantile thing to do."

"That's what I thought too." Eros plopped down onto a cerise divan made of cumulus clouds. "So how can I be of service to you?"

She smiled. "You know me too well."

"I do."

She adjusted her crown of gold and joined him on the divan. "I am losing worshippers. My altars are covered in cold ashes. No sculptor will build a statue of me."

"And how can I amend that?"

"The person for whom my worshippers are forsaking me is a mere mortal girl. She is said to rival even…" Aphrodite paused as if she tasted something unsavory. "She is said to be very beautiful and she does not wish to marry no matter how many suitors come to her. I need her to fall in love with a hideous, contemptible man, who will take her as a wife and will finally put a stop to her frivolousness."

"I feel like we've done this before. Care to try something more fun with this girl? Perhaps make her fall in love with your statue and destroy her beauty with her own hands for your sake?"

Aphrodite raised her eyebrows. "That is intriguing." But then she frowned. "However, it would make me look rather cruel. No, give her a husband, then she won't be nearly as interesting. And all the better if he's the controlling kind."

"Are you certain?"

"As much as your schemes amuse me, I don't have the patience for this one."

"Fine," Eros drawled, stretching out like a petulant child. "I shall bore myself for your sake."

Aphrodite reached out and took his chin into her elegant fingers. "My beautiful, sweet boy wait until you're as old as me and you'll see what it means to lose even the smallest bit of adoration." Behind the raw beauty in her eyes hid a vile viciousness. A viciousness he never forgot about. After all, it was a part of him too. If it wasn't for Anteros, Eros would have had much less qualms about causing harm with his arrows. Not that he had too many qualms now.

"A catastrophe," he said.

"Precisely." She smiled. "So just shoot her and be done with it."

Eros sighed. "So be it." He spread out his hands, conjuring up his bow and arrows. "One dysfunctional couple, coming right up."

III Boredom and Apricot Spears

It was dawn and Psyche was bored and alone. But instead of going out to walk the length of the shore, looking for nymphs hiding in the depthless tides of the ocean, she had to wait in her room.

As a young child, Psyche would get into all of her sisters' things in search of something interesting. Then she'd get scolded, after which they'd all run out to the beach, their *yiayia* shouting behind them. Now, there was decorum to follow and only one sister whose things Psyche could scour through, not that she ever did. Her other sister was lost to the life of matrimony. There was very little adventure to be had for a princess of a small kingdom.

"Save for adventure in marriage," her *yiayia* would say with a wink.

But Psyche wasn't so certain. Her elder sister, Leda, was married and if her stories were anything to go by, Psyche did not think marriage would be an adventure. More of an obligation. And an uncomfortable one at that.

"That's because Leda does not love her husband," Elara would say. "And can you blame her? He might be rich but even Hephaestus would run away screaming from the sight of his face."

"Hush now," *yiayia* would say.

"But you shouldn't have the same difficulty," Elara would say with a smile. "You are beautiful."

And then their *yiayia* would usher them to eat or walk in the gardens from where they could watch the royal guard train.

If only Psyche could walk now. It's been two weeks since she could even venture outside. And all because of her father's outrageous plot.

The kingdom had been struggling with money for years and her father had got it in his head to spread the rumor of Psyche's beauty far and wide, so that men would come from all over the place and pay a good sum of money to look at her. And come they did, though they were never permitted to see her up close. She always showed herself from her window. The men saw her flowing raven hair and a splendid *peplos* that draped over her curves and they were satisfied. After all she had the fame of being the most beautiful girl in all of Greece, and the truth about whether she actually was beautiful or not didn't matter. Titles and reputations were worth more. Much more.

Now, Psyche just had to wait for a wealthy husband to come and make an offer of marriage to her. The offers thus far have been too low for her father's liking. Not that she minded the wait. Marriage wasn't exactly what she had in mind for herself.

So, to pass the time until the men began gathering under her window, Psyche reached under her *kline* and got a spear she'd made from a fallen branch of an apricot tree.

"If only I was free again," she said to herself as she lifted the spear above her head and thrust it forward. "But no, after this there'll be marriage and children and more senseless rules." She spun it in her fingers and attacked invisible opponents. As she imagined the beasts, the monsters, and the men who loitered below the castle, Psyche swung the apricot spear with such force that it flew at the wall next to the window and left an indent on a painstakingly painted panorama of their city-state.

"*Kunops,*" Psyche swore.

If only she could be free again, she thought, it'd be so wonderful. As she went to pick up the stick, Psyche felt a strange presence. When she spun around, stick in hand, she saw no one.

Great, was she going to start hallucinating from boredom now?

IV Evil Spirits and Dropped Arrows

The next morning, Eros flew over the coast to a palace precariously built atop a cliff that overlooked the stormy ocean. He soared above the grounds, invisible to mortal eyes, and studied his surroundings. Anteros's arrows were sharpened and ready; but his hands itched to draw his own arrows and watch the mortals go mad.

Boring.

He saw a handful of men at the foot of the palace. It was more admirers than most mortals saw in their lifetime, but it was not even enough to leave a dent in his mother's following. She really did worry too much.

His task for now was simple: Find a tolerably hideous man. It wasn't hard to do. There were quite a few of them here. A bald one with protruding teeth, who would follow her around like a love forlorn cyclops. Another one was old and oiled in sweat and he seemed like the kind to lock her away in his house and never let her out. And then there was one with angry brows and foul-smelling feet. He seemed the kind to take joy in beating his wives.

"What would a princess like?" Eros mused out loud. He circled the crowd a few times until he spotted someone. "Ah, you will do."

Eros flew over the man and hung above him upside down, studying his face. He had thin hair, weak physique, and a sickly pallor. He did have nice eyes and a respect for royalty. At least, their love would be one filled with the selfless wholesomeness of Anteros's arrows and would last into their old age.

Boring.

Yes, he'd do perfectly. Aphrodite wouldn't even think to suspect a thing.

Once that target had been identified, Eros went to search for Psyche. This was also not very difficult to do. Most of the men flocked under the left tower and so all Eros had to do was fly up to the window. But as soon as he was inside, something flew at him. He barely managed to jump out of the way as a branch hit the wall with a thud. A girl swore, quite colorfully in fact, and stalked over to the stick. She studied the cavity in the wall with a frustrated frown.

This was not quite what Eros expected. It was like running into Athena instead of a shy water nymph. He didn't like being surprised. Surprising others, yes, but being surprised, not so much. Eros hovered near the ceiling so he wouldn't get hit again. He might have been invisible, but he was quite sure the sharpened point would hurt him.

Then the girl, Psyche, spun around and cast a wary look around the room.

Eros smiled. Most mortals could feel something when a god was with them and it was amusing to watch them squirm, though the fun wore out quickly. Once again, he studied his target.

Psyche was not the most beautiful girl he'd ever seen; she didn't even come in tenth. There were goddesses on Olympus who would put her appearance to shame, but she wasn't unpleasant. She had long, black hair coiled into a thick braid. Her *peplos* was modest and deftly embroidered. The body underneath was young and shapely. She moved with a decided purpose and Eros liked that too, though there wasn't far she could go with that purpose. At least not in this kingdom, nor with Aphrodite as her enemy.

"Who is in here?" she called, as if gods had made it a habit to reply to her. Then she raised the stick and sliced through the air. "Get out evil spirit."

The stick came near Eros's wings but missed. He couldn't help but laugh. He rarely saw such antics on display.

"Or at least…" she began but then a knock came at her door.

Eros still watched the girl as she pursed her lips and rushed to hide her weapon. When the door opened, two women came in, one old, one young.

"Ai, look at this girl, you haven't even brushed your hair," the older woman said.

"Does she ever," the other girl said.

"Yes, I do."

"Once in a blue moon perhaps."

And together they began undoing Psyche's hair.

"Anybody new?" Psyche asked.

"Nobody your father approves of," the woman said.

There was silence.

So, this was why she wasn't married yet.

Well, it would all change today when she fell in love with a bride groom.

Eros flew over to the window and found the man in the crowd. He took out an arrow and placed it on the bow. As he did, there was a sharp cry behind him.

The arrow slipped out of his hand.

It fell for what felt like an eternity. But then the tip of it pricked his foot. Eros's heart froze as a fine warmth spread through him. It was almost like hearing a new language, a strange, beautiful concoction of foreign sounds and new sensations, and understanding it perfectly. It was an enigma. A promise sweeter than ambrosia.

No.

No, no, no.

But even as his mind protested, Eros turned and saw Psyche. He supposed he should have been relieved it hadn't been the old woman he saw first, but he could barely think through the ache in his chest. All he could think about was Psyche and the stars burning in her sorrowful eyes.

No.

Eros staggered back, running into her wooden *kline* next to the window. His wings spread out though he wasn't outside yet and collapsed back with a panicked flutter when they met the hard walls.

He was unsettled.

He had to get away.

Far away.

By the time he squeezed out the window, Eros was not himself. Some gods whispered that he was not born of Aphrodite and Ares at all but of Chaos. In that instant, he believed it. Because even as he took flight, letting Zephyrus guide the way, the uncontrollable madness within him grew.

He stumbled into his abode, frightened and uncertain.

Instead of hiding his quiver and arrows with his magic, Eros chucked them across the cloud cover.

Anteros's arrow be damned.

Cherubs surrounded him, questions on their lips.

"Go away," he said. "All of you, get out."

They did, melting away into the wisps of greying clouds.

Eros put his face into his hands and tried to reason his way through this. Nobody knew except him. Nobody. And nobody had to find out.

He merely had to return to her and finish Aphrodite's request. Eros glanced at the scattered arrows. He stood up and forced himself to pick them up as Psyche had picked up her makeshift spear.

And then he realized he was thinking of that damned mortal girl.

He was thinking of her fondly.

Damn her.

Damn him.

V A Test Unpassed

Eros returned to Psyche's room that evening.

He flew under the guise of darkness, his heart beating in a long-forgotten pattern of unease.

A single man was idling under her tower, showing astounding enthusiasm and dedication. He was the same man Eros had marked out as a target earlier.

"Perfect," Eros said, even though it felt far from it. He'd hoped there'd be no one here, he hoped it would allow him to defer this for another day, to come here again, but there was someone, which meant he had to at least try. He drew an arrow as he approached Psyche's window.

He thought of way he could draw her to the window when he came face to face with her instead. She was hiding behind the wall, occasionally stealing peeks outside.

Eros startled.

She really was an odd human. An illogical one. What was she even doing?

It doesn't matter.

Eros drew the arrow on his bow and aimed it at her. The man began walking away down the shoreline. Eros had to act fast.

Now.

His hands trembled from the strain.

Do it.

The man was growing smaller and smaller.

With an irritated sigh, Eros put the bow down and stared after him. And when he looked at Psyche, he knew that he couldn't do it. Even if he returned tomorrow or the day after or a decade from now, he wouldn't be able to do it.

Sensing something, Psyche looked around. Her eyes widened and she went still, as if waiting. Her breaths went shallow. But she didn't say anything, all her bravado gone in the night. Afraid, Eros realized. She was afraid.

So mortal of them to fear the dark.
Eros couldn't torment her or himself any longer. So he looked at her, one chaste glance, and flew away.

VI Thank Gods for No Suitors?

Reputations really did precede themselves and scarcity fed desire.

Soon, dozens of men were coming to look at Psyche every day. The word of her beauty had even reached the prince of the wealthy neighboring kingdom. He came with an enviable procession. He was young and beautiful but most important of all, he was rich. Her father was in Elysium from happiness.

The only problem was that when the prince saw Psyche, he did not make an offer of marriage. At best, he was pleased by her beauty if not smitten. He stared at her, scrutinizing her face. However, no matter how much Psyche smiled and played the demure girl her parents wanted her to be, the prince did not fall at her feet. Did not throw all his money at the kingdom. The thought didn't even seem to cross his mind. His black curls lifted in the breeze, his eyes drank her in, and his smile remained just as unaffected.

Psyche shared a worried glance with her mother.

Time passed.

The sun set behind the precipice of the ocean, coloring the palace in dulcet colors.

The prince left the way he came, parting a confused crowd of suitors with his procession.

Psyche had seen how disappointed the men had been when the prince was admitted into the palace and now, she saw uncertainty bloom on their faces as he left. This was the danger with reputations. They were sand castles, subject to the whim of the tides.

"Now nobody will want her," her mother told her father. "And you'll be known as the king who lied."

"Don't talk to me that way," he shouted.

"I will talk as I please. You didn't listen to me when I warned you."

He moved to hit her and both Psyche and Elara took a step to stop him. Before his palm connected with her cheek, he stopped. He straightened his toga and took a deep breath. "Do not talk back to me that way. There are still plenty men left."

And so over the course of the next few days, those who remained were invited to see Psyche. None fell in love with her. At least not enough to marry her.

Psyche, who had been dreading being proposed to, now dreaded the opposite. Ever since she had been young, she'd heard how beautiful she was and how marriage wouldn't be a problem for her. And she'd believed it. She'd always thought of it as something inevitable but not impossible. Now, doubts began to shadow her dreams, for what was a girl without a husband? What would she be? The answer was as loud as the crashing of the ocean. *Nothing.*

Days passed and even the poorest of the suitors did not wish to marry her.

Psyche's *yiayia* brushed her hair as the moon graced the sky.

The last of the suitors had left without proposing to her and her father was furious.

Psyche felt like nothing. Even though she knew she was wrong.

She imagined her family was so disappointed that they'd abandon her, even her *yiayia,* and Psyche would grow old alone on a bare strip of land.

"You won't leave me, will you?" she asked her *yiayia.*

"Never," her *yiayia* replied and there was such a fierceness in her voice that Psyche believed it.

Then a servant burst into Psyche's room and said, "Elara was proposed to."

Psyche blinked, the words coming to her as if they'd been spoken under water.

Her *yiayia* helped her up and together they went to the great hall. Torches burned with a merry glow as one of the wealthy merchants who had come to the palace yesterday discussed business with the king and his advisors. It was rare that men and women were allowed in the same room but tonight was a special occasion.

Elara ran up to them, her eyes wide. She was nineteen summers old and so she was ready for marriage, but still Psyche saw the inkling of worry in her eyes. But the merchant was handsome and wealthy besides. Psyche took her sister's hands and their *yiayia* kissed her forehead.

A long while passed. Spring turned to summer and Elara had her wedding. It was one befit a king's daughter and she looked happy. Psyche was happy too. How could she not be? It was her sister. Psyche's own fortune might have been cursed, but Elara's wasn't, and she could at least take joy in that.

And she did.

But as the wedding passed and summer turned to autumn, still nobody proposed to Psyche. That's when her parents got worried.

"We should take her to Apollo's oracle," Psyche's mother proposed. She was a wise queen, at least wiser than the king, and so naturally her idea was dismissed. But she had a way of eating away at her husband until he gave in and finally, on the brink of days when warm summer breezes gave way to winter's harsh winds, it was decided. They would go to the oracle.

VII Anteros Gives Advice and Eros Listens

Eros, the god of love, was officially closed for business.

He would not leave his cocoon of clouds, having stocked up on enough ambrosia to last a century. His cherubs had to double down on their work in order to make enough humans fall in love, but without Eros, the numbers were quickly plummeting into an icy chasm. A chasm where less and less people got together quickly enough to sustain a worshipping population.

Anteros did what he could but his arrows took time to grow into something more. Though they seemed to have worked too well on Eros.

Anteros regarded the clouds his brother had made. They were an angry grey but not impenetrable.

He pushed his way inside.

There he found Eros sleeping.

When Eros had told him about what happened, Anteros told him he'd think about a solution. But unlike Eros's arrows, Anteros's didn't fade with time. If anything, they only grew stronger. And so, thought as he might, Anteros could not come up with any way to help his brother out of this mess.

Really, it was Demeter all over again, when she'd refused to do her duty after Persephone was taken and their world stopped functioning as it should. All the gods were important and if one neglected their duties, the world could not go on as normal.

And now that Anteros thought about it, Eros had been one to blame for that fiasco too.

He shook Eros awake. "Are you intent on sleeping this century away?"

"Yes," he groaned, half-asleep. A shaft of sunlight fell on his golden features.

"Get up."

Eros pushed him away. "Tell me what you came up with."

"Marry her," Anteros said.

The golden god sat up with a frown rivaling Ares's.

"Hear me out," Anteros started.

"No, I won't. I'm the God of Desire. The God of Lust. The God of Love. Capital letters all. I don't *marry*."

"Your other option is to wait until she dies."

Eros wavered, his eyes cast downward. He looked genuinely distraught at the thought.

"It'll be a long few decades," Anteros said. "But if you marry her, you can make them go faster."

"I don't want them to go faster," Eros muttered. "I want to forget her. Maybe I can visit the Underworld and take a sip from Lethes."

"Are you mad?"

"You would know."

"Yes, I would know," Anteros said. "That's a daft solution."

"I didn't hear anything better from you."

The clouds darkened and a sudden smell of rain enveloped them.

Anteros blew out a puff of air. "Then just go talk to her."

"Talk to her?"

"Yes, get to know her. Become friends, become lovers. No marriage."

Eros straightened, clearly liking this idea more. "What about mother?"

"Stop acting like a child. Mother doesn't have to find out. Besides, she's already furious with you for failing to do what she asked, so it would actually be beneficial for all of us if she didn't find out."

Eros contemplated the idea but then he put a hand over his eyes with a groan. "I can't just use Psyche like that."

Anteros couldn't help but smile. This was not like Eros at all. He liked him so much better this way.

"You wouldn't be using her if you married her," he said. "Mother won't let anyone marry her anyway."

"What?"

"That was her plan of retaliation."

Eros rolled his eyes.

"So you can marry Psyche in secret and keep her as a wife in a palace on earth. Just don't show yourself to her. We don't want her recognizing your face and going to your altars to call on you, shall you leave. If she does, then Aphrodite might find out and that'll be a whole another disaster. Not to mention the gods you've offended. Once Psyche dies, time will heal the wound from the arrow."

Eros looked miserable.

"Or if you're really nice to Hades, you can go visit her in the Underworld. Maybe put in a good word for her at the Elysium Fields."

"For a god of selfless love, you are cruel," Eros said.

"I know." Anteros patted his brother's shoulder. "Now stop moping, the world is awaiting your return."

VIII Oracle Speaks of Monsters

The inner temple at Delphi was dark, illuminated only with torches of watery light. This was one of the most renowned temples built for Apollo and it was the center of the world. If anybody could help shed light on Psyche's problem, it was the Oracle of Delphi.

The fumes swirled in the dimness, carving an ache into Psyche's head. Her parents were on either side of her. It was deathly quiet.

The priestess waited for them in the center of the room, surrounded by tall torches staked into the ground. She held a bowl with a clear liquid and a branch of laurel. Her garments, which had been the color of a warm hearth and wood, were now covered by a blood-red cloth that snaked over her body like tongues of fire. Her eyes were clouded white.

"Ask thy question," she said. Her voice was unnaturally deep and it felt as if more than one person was speaking, though there was no one else in the room.

Psyche's father cleared his throat. "Nobody will marry Psyche, my youngest daughter, O great priestess. Tell us how we can amend that. Tell us if we have offended the gods?"

The Oracle was silent, and her eyes moved back and forth. Psyche's mouth was dry, her mind racing over everything that could have been wrong with her. Maybe the men didn't like her liberal behavior and, sensing the adventurous glint in her manners, ran to those who would be less of a bother. Or maybe they were disappointed in her appearance after all.

The Oracle laughed, bringing Psyche back into reality. There was more than one voice in that sound. It was as if Apollo himself was laughing through her. "Offended, yes," she said. "And as a result, your daughter is to wed a monster neither human nor god can tame. Leave her on top of a hill and forget you ever had a daughter named Psyche."

Her mother gasped.

Psyche felt as if she'd swallowed dirty water.

"What happens if we don't?" her mother asked.

"The gods will forsake your kingdom in times most difficult."

The word *monster* kept ringing out in the silence.

IX Building Mortal Palaces

Eros floated over a palace with elegant spires and enormous staircases.

For a god who was used to walking on clouds, this earthen construction seemed to lack a certain finesse. Everything about it felt crude and heavy no matter how much he tried to fix it. But it was better than anything Eros had seen during his travels and that was something, considering how many castles and palaces he *had* seen. He was even a little proud of his creation.

Yes, it would do for Psyche.

Psyche.

Even her name made his heart constrict with anticipation. He wanted to give her the best. He even thought of making her a goddess, but Aphrodite would kill her before Eros could blink, and Zeus would use her to force Eros to do his bidding. Eros couldn't have that. So, he had created a palace in the middle of an island with expansive stretch of emerald hills and azure skies and made sure to staff it with a few of his cupids, all enchanted to be invisible to the mortal eye.

It was the best he could offer. If she'd have him. And if she didn't… well, he hadn't thought of that.

Eros landed at the entrance and steadied his breath.

He hadn't realized how strong his brother's arrows were. Made to last indeed.

But with every passing day, Eros was becoming less and less angry at his own stupidity and more and more grateful for his mistake.

After all, wasn't it fitting for someone who was renowned for being the god of love to have loved at least once?

No.

No, it wasn't. He wasn't in love. This was temporary. After a few nights with her, all would pass.

Yes.

A few nights of her embraces was all he needed. And then everything would return to normal. It had to.

So, he summoned Zephyrus and flew to Psyche.

He thought of a thousand things to say. Of ancient poetry that touched the soul and of robust prose that inspired the heart. Of simple greetings and of complicated explanations. He was on his twentieth variant of an introduction when he noticed a procession of people clad in black. Torches winked in the lavender twilight, women sobbed into their shawls, and men cried into their sleeves. With a leaden heart, Eros slid in among them.

Every bad thing that could cross his mind did. That is until he heard the whispers about Apollo's prophecy and learned that they'd left Psyche up on a hill to wait for a monster.

A monster.

Eros grimaced. Apollo was still mad at him then. But he wasn't wrong

Eros rose up into the air, joining Zephyrus once again. He flew over knolls of olive green. The velvety night blanketed them in sheer darkness by the time he reached the hill.

On top of the highest one, he expected to see a beautiful, shivering girl sitting mournfully but dutifully as she awaited her fate. Instead, he found someone pacing back and force, grumbling quite an array of indignant curses.

Eros flew closer.

X Winds of Change

Psyche was not one to blindly listen to prophecies, but this was the one prophecy she couldn't afford to ignore. Her whole kingdom was at stake.

Her tear-swollen eyes stung as she walked back and forth, her feet slipping on rocks. Her throat was still coarse from crying. The words *yiayia* were bitter on her tongue. Her grandmother hadn't wanted to leave either, so she'd had to be dragged away by guards. Psyche's heart hurt remembering the anguish on her weathered face. But there was nothing either of them could've done.

The wind was cold. It cut to the bone. She remembered seeing a gathering of giant boulders on the way. They would shield her from the worst of the wind. But each time Psyche thought of leaving her spot on top of the hill, she stopped herself because she was afraid the monster wouldn't be able to find her if she did. She couldn't even hope for him not to come, because she knew it would doom her kingdom. And so the wind kept slicing through her and she kept moving back and forth to warm up.

Suddenly, Psyche's foot slipped, and she found herself tripping. She was prepared to fall but that moment never came as some force held her suspended midair.

She frowned and then she was flying.

The stars were closer to her, a mantle of twinkling lights. The wind spun her around and now she was upright, floating over a patchwork of greens and browns and dark yellows. But no, it wasn't a patchwork, it was land. Farmland, mountains, woods. She didn't even notice the cold as the wind carried her to an unknown destination.

What if I'm dead?

Psyche considered her arms and the rippling sound of her bridal gown. Her hair and veil were in her mouth, as was dust and grit. It smelled of icy wind. Her eyes still stung.

She *couldn't* be dead.

Then hallucinating.

Psyche could barely enjoy the flight with all of the questions plaguing her. Curiosity was perhaps another curse.

Then, the wind carried her over an enormous palace and lowered her onto a balcony overlooking a silvery lake. Stars were reflected on its surface and as soon as Psyche's feet touched the floor, warm glowing lights joined them. The palace came to life behind her.

Psyche turned around.

Torches shaped in impossibly elegant curves grew out of stone walls and illuminated the place with golden light. Psyche had never seen so much light in one place. It felt like a breath of daylight was caught in a bubble under the ocean of night.

She rushed inside, going straight to a table stuffed with food. Fruits, vegetables, breads, all was there glistening with glazes and syrups. She was starving until she spotted a pomegranate and her fears flared to life. Hades had lured Persephone to the Underworld and made her stay there with a few pomegranate seeds, hadn't he? If Psyche tasted the food, she might get trapped here for eternity, not that it mattered. Still, she stepped away from the table and glanced around through her veil. "Is this the castle of my monstrous husband to be?" she asked, her heart pounding.

The answer came right away, though she hadn't expected it. *It's your castle.* But it sounded more like a chorus of children.

"Who said that?"

Your servants.

Psyche looked around but the room remained empty. This was not good.

You're hungry and tired. Eat, rest.

A door opened on a smooth stone surface leading to a bed.

"Where is the one Apollo's prophecy spoke of?" she asked, feeling her own quivering, warm breath on the veil.

Another, deeper voice said, "I am here." It was a beautiful voice, filled with an aching melody of longing. He sounded like a youth, not a monster.

Psyche swallowed. "Why am I the one chosen to wed you?"

"Fates have willed it so."

Psyche tried to nod, to reply, but fear was choking her.

"Do you not want to?" he asked when she said nothing.

"I don't want to marry a monster," Psyche replied, "I haven't seen. Who are you?"

"You can't know that."

"And yet I am expected to be your wife?"

"No. Nothing is expected of you."

She glanced at the room with the bed. Clearly, something was expected or else she wouldn't have been there. And the Oracle wouldn't have prophesied a marriage.

"You're here," the voice said, moving across the room and coming to a stop in front of her. "Because you were in need of a home."

Psyche stepped back, unnerved.

Then her veil moved to reveal her face. She saw the room more crisply without the embroidery of the veil to obstruct her view. Psyche squinted into every shadow only to be met with ordinary things that resided in them. Chairs, unlit torches, vases.

The invisible presence moved away. She knew because she suddenly felt colder.

"And when…" she started wanting to know when they'd be wed but thought better of it. If he wasn't forcing her, she needn't remind him just yet. So she said, "And when will you show yourself?"

An apple floated up to her. "I won't."

Psyche took it, her skin coming into contact with something shockingly warm. Hot even.

"The supper is for you," he said with a rough voice. "Good night."

"Good night," was all she could mutter in return.

XI A Hurricane with Edges

Eros could not do it. If it had been one of his own arrows, maybe. But it wasn't.

He thought he could force Psyche to marry him, but when he saw her, standing there fearfully, he couldn't do it. And it's not as if he could make her fall in love with an arrow because then he would have to show himself to her and that was forbidden. If he did, it would turn into a dark, seething mess he would have to be untangling long after her bones turned to dust.

So, he did the next best thing. He flew away.

The following day, Eros told Anteros that the plan hadn't worked and threw himself into work and trickery, wandering the world, amending for his long absence, and making gods suffer. A month must have passed by the time he returned to his abode. He was tired, hungry, and irritated at all the love he had spread. And to put the olive on top, he found Ares waiting for him at home instead of a quiet day of drinking ambrosia over the coastline.

The god of war was a menace. He was made of hurricanes with sharp edges and a single moment with him could cut deeply. He could make you want to lust for the gory glory of war like no other. He reminded others of the darkness within them and made them into monsters. Not that Eros needed to be made into one.

Eros landed in his great hall of clouds that overlooked the world. "The prodigal father pays a visit at last."

Ares smiled, leaning back into the clouds which were black where he touched them in his shroud of all kinds of skins, animal and human. "A war is coming."

"Right to the point."

"You know I dislike small talk."

Eros grimaced. "Haven't you heard I make love, not war?"

"*You* may make love but *love* makes war."

"Really? I was under the impression you were in charge of that."

"What's wrong? I thought you'd be thrilled."

"I'm mildly diverted." Eros forced himself to sit across from Ares. He may have enjoyed some aspects of war but the carnage and torture he always found distasteful "Let's stop making small talk, tell me what it is you want."

Ares inclined his head. "The gods are dividing."

Eros shrugged. Gods divided and argued and made war almost as often as Aphrodite got mad at beautiful mortals. And Olympus crackled under the bored hatred of the gods long after the fighting seized, making easy targets for Eros. "What's the reason this time?"

"Zeus disrespected Artemis by abducting one her priestesses."

"Oh," Eros said. With his own mishaps, Eros had forgotten all about Zeus. He'd heard that he was chasing goddesses and assumed all was normal.

"Oh?" Ares chuckled. "I'll take it that was your handiwork?"

"If you're suggesting I did it with malicious intent, you're wrong."

"Am I?"

Eros looked away. The sun was setting. "Apollo is taking her side, I assume?"

"Naturally."

"And you're with Zeus?"

"Only because Athena sided with Artemis first."

Why did Eros even bother asking? When Ares was in a war, he didn't care which side he was on, so long as he was not on the same side as Athena and as long as there was slaughter. Eros usually joined the wars because it made for a charged environment for love to bloom and sometimes, he also liked to curb the pain of the mortals by giving them something else to think about. He'd always thought it was better to go mad from love than torture. Now he wasn't sure. But then again, he'd never been seriously injured before.

"Alright," Eros said, "send word when I'm needed."

"Don't look so forlorn." Ares stood up. "It is what it is. You might as well enjoy it."

Eros gave a dismissive nod and once he was alone, collapsed into the clouds.

XII Flying Through Twilight

For the first week, Psyche kept to her rooms, frightened and sad. However, when her host, and she preferred to think of him as her host and not her betrothed, didn't come back, Psyche got bolder. Curiosity bloomed life back into her.

At first, she was afraid being away from home would be unbearable but the first month in this enormous, forgotten palace had been nothing but a big adventure. She had explored the gardens, of which there were four; the halls, of which there were seven; and the rooms, of which there were at least a hundred. But there was only so much enjoyment one could derive from marvels without anybody to share it with. And Psyche had reached that limit.

Now, as Psyche walked amidst the tall colonnades that rose up like ancient old trees in golden sunlight, she thought of her sisters. If only they were here. How much fun would they have?

"Could I have more wine and bread, please," Psyche said to her invisible servants.

Of course.

At first, they too were an adventure. But now they were a simple part of life, especially since they didn't really talk to her.

The wine and bread were brought to her when she sat down on the steps down to the garden with the apricot trees. There was a swath of shade towards the bottom and a lovely view dappled with sunlight.

She dipped the barley bread into the goblet and ate, thinking of nothing in particular. It would probably take her another month to get truly bored. Then she'd begin thinking of the borders of this isolated kingdom for one.

A plump apricot caught her eye from one of the trees. It was golden and beautiful, and would no doubt make for a perfect end to her lunch. So, Psyche stood up and went over to the tree. Gathering her skirts, she began to climb. At least there was no one who scolded her for behaving inappropriately. She could run, climb, and yell to her heart's content. And if the servants didn't approve, well, she couldn't see them.

She grabbed onto the first branch and pulled herself up. The bark was rough beneath her fingers. Butterflies fluttered from fruit to fruit, their thin wings catching the afternoon light in breathtaking displays.

Higher and higher she went.

Leaves got caught in her hair. The fruit was almost within her reach.

Then suddenly, something lifted her up and she almost fell. At the last moment she managed to grab onto a branch and hold on. Once she was standing steadily, she looked around. The invisible servants never touched her or lifted her up, so it could only be her host. Fear and excitement coursed through her.

"You should give me a warning before you do that," Psyche said.

There was no reply and she thought she had imagined the wind.

"Hello. Are you there?"

"I thought you needed help," the deep, melodious voice said. It was as if he stood right next to her. Close enough to touch.

"I can climb trees quite well, thank you," she replied, plucking off the apricot that hung right above her nose.

"My bad."

"Don't worry about it." She lowered herself onto the branch and sat down. In order to hide her anxiety, she began to eat the fruit.

"You're not afraid of me?"

Psyche was, she was terrified, but something told her that if he'd wanted to hurt her, he would have. So, she tried to be nice. "Not at all. You seem like a nice invisible host.

"Host?"

"I don't know what else to call you."

There was a moment of silence. "Host is fine."

"Alright," she said, "so tell me, how have you been?"

The branch shifted and Psyche felt him sit beside her. "Occupied."

"With what?"

"Work."

"You work?"

"Everybody works."

"Why would you need to work when you have a palace like this?"

"I get bored," he said.

"Oh yes, I suppose being invisible *must* get quite lonely," she said teasingly.

"Probably as lonely as sitting in this palace," he said.

Psyche looked up, surprised.

"I didn't mean to abandon you like this," he went on and then cleared his throat.

"Women are made to endure worse," she said to the thin air. There was a soft smell of apricots around her. Apricots and rain and fresh air. "I thought I'd have to endure worse."

"Wed to a monster, yes," he said. "I can imagine."

Psyche put the apricot in her pocket, her pulse increasing at what she was about to say. "Can I ask you a favor?"

"You can."

"I want to fly," she said, looking up at the sky. "Is that possible?"

"Aren't you afraid?"

"I'm not. It's the closest I'll get to seeing the world and feeling the rush of adventure."

The weight on the branch shifted as if he got off it.

"Wait, don't leave," she said, casting her gaze around blindly. "We don't have to—"

"Give me your hand," he said.

Psyche extended it into the empty air and felt warm fingers wrap around it. Then an arm curled around her waist and before she could consider how human it felt, they were airborne.

Her heart racketed as the sky surrounded her. A whole new world of azure and indigo opened up, blinking at her in wonderment. Psyche's urge was to close her eyes, but she kept them wide open.

How many times had she looked up and wondered what it'd be like to be a bird? Too many. Now, she knew. It was unforgettable. The wind caressed her hair and a terror unfolded, dark and thrilling, and bloomed into sheer bliss. Her heart and stomach dropped with every swoop and rise and spin. Her lips ached from smiling. Her eyes stung but she didn't mind.

They flew until the blues gave way to violets and lavenders. She saw that she was on an island with the ocean all around. The way the sunlight played with the waves was mesmerizing, but it also reminded her that she was indeed in a cage.

After sunset, he set her down amidst drooping bushes of lilacs, but didn't let go. His hands lingered on her hips and hers around his neck.

They were quiet and in the dark cobalt night, she thought she could make out his outline.

XIII When the God of War Calls

"Are you alright?" he asked, breathless.

"Yes," she said, an excited smile still on her lips. "But where in the world did you find such a large island?"

For a pathetic human, Psyche was brave. And Eros didn't think it was just the arrow speaking. He found her forthrightness familiar. It was as if he was talking to someone he'd known for an eternity.

"It's a big world," Eros said. In the darkness, her eyes shone brightly.

"How big?"

"May you find out one day."

Then a cherub floated over to him. "Master, a message is waiting for you."

Psyche glanced around, surprised, and stepped away.

He didn't hold on to her, didn't stop her.

"You're leaving," she said.

"I'll be back sooner this time. Do you like books?" He turned to his cherubs and said. "Show her the library."

"Um, well, I never learned to read," she said.

Right. He kept forgetting about men's desperate means of protecting their power.

"They'll teach you," Eros said. "Good night."

And he took flight, feeling as if he was leaving his heart behind with her.

At his abode, he found a message and Anteros.

"You're back," Eros said, accepting a burning skull from a cherub.

"I had to." Anteros nodded at the skull. "I heard there was to be a war."

Eros crushed the skull in his hand and a mass of smoke escaped into the great hall. Its deadly grey pallor was of great contrast to the soft white clouds. It showed the city of Corinth harboring Athenians. And Aetolians, who worshipped Ares, were heading there for a blood bath. Hatred was already in their hearts.

"Join me?" Eros asked.

For all of Anteros's selfless love, he, like all the other gods, could cause great damage. Those who have cruelly spurned others were especially at stake.

Anteros swallowed. "Does it always have to be this way?"

"It is what it is," Eros said, summoning his bows, both the golden and the leaden ones. Anteros followed suit and together they flew to Corinth.

By the time they reached the city, it was under siege. It reeked of burnt bodies and blood. Pools of boiled oil spread under moaning half-corpses.

Athena stood atop the wall and Ares charged with a loud, thunderous army. Neither of them had noticed Eros and Anteros. Using their obliviousness, Eros shot the guards at the door and they fell in love with whoever they saw first. But it didn't end at that. Eros hadn't just shot them with one arrow but multiple, so their desire tore them apart as they got distracted and ignored their captain's orders. Now that he knew how much love could hurt, he pitied them. But this was war and men were expendable. After all, they'd die and go to Hades.

Eros would have shot Athena too, but he knew he'd only be wasting his arrows. She could evade anything.

Anteros had moved on to shoot the ones who oversaw the cauldrons with the hot oil.

Athena turned her head and saw Eros. But it was too late. Ares and his army had used the distraction of the guards to shoot them down and reach the door.

Artemis joined Athena and aimed at Eros, but he too was a good evader.

A loud crash sounded as the doors opened and the Aetolians spilled into Corinth. Then there were screams. Desperate and terrified.

Cruelty was a part of life, Eros knew that. He had never pitied humans before, but knowing Psyche, well, it changed his perspective. He couldn't leave the humans to suffer. So despite Anteros's warning, Eros flew into Corinth, and made sure the terrified people were oblivious to pain as their life bled out of them.

XIV There Be Monsters There

A week passed since her little adventure. And true to his word, her host came earlier. But this time, he didn't appear in golden sunlight trailing the smell of rain and wind behind him. He came in the dead of the night, shadowed by the coppery stench of blood.

She felt him collapse on the bed beside her.

His strenuous breaths filled the silence.

"Torches," she said, sitting up. The lights came on and though she saw no one on the bed, she could see drops of blood. "What's wrong? Are you hurt?"

"No," the familiar voice said.

Psyche reached out but his face was closer than she thought so she ended up hitting him.

"Ow," he groaned.

"Sorry."

He shifted away without saying a word.

"What happened?"

"I'm tired."

"And do you always bleed when you're tired?"

"It's not my blood."

The words sank in with a vicious chill and split open her healing veins of fear. But Psyche remained where she was, half-afraid to move, half-curious to know.

"I shouldn't have come," he said. The bed creaked.

"No, wait." Psyche stood up too and rounded it to his side but there was no one there. She snarled in frustration. Would it kill him to explain things? It wasn't as if her head was going to break.

"I'm still here," he said.

Psyche jumped, her heart in her throat. She turned to where the voice came from. The bed chamber was quite big and there was a table by one of the walls with jugs of water and goblets. She watched a goblet be lifted into the air.

"How was I supposed to know?" she said, her face warming at her outburst. "Besides, why can't I see you or anybody in this palace?"

"Because I don't want you to."

"You can't be that hideous."

He gave a small laugh. "Worse."

"So," she began walking back and forth. "I can't ask you about the blood?"

"I'd rather forget about it."

If it were that easy.

"Let's talk about something else," he said, the goblet floating closer to her.

Psyche frowned. "I thought you were tired. You need to rest."

He passed by her. She felt him *and* saw the goblet. "What I need is a distraction," he said.

Psyche didn't turn around, wary of his insinuation. "A distraction?"

"Let's talk about your reading lessons."

She relaxed, her nerves unwinding. She turned to face him. "They're dull, for now," she said. "I can barely read a sentence." But she couldn't wait to learn more so she could unlock the adventures that hid in those ancient scrolls. If only she could stop getting distracted by her hikes towards the edge of the island. Not that she ever made it far. The invisible servants made sure of that.

"Is there anything else that interests you?" he asked.

Psyche thought back to her old life. She wondered what she'd filled her hours with there. Talking to her sisters, learning to cook from her *yiayia,* exploring the shore, watching the guards practice. It wasn't much and yet time had flown. "I've always wanted to learn archery," she said, thinking of the royal guard and their training. "And I want to see the ocean."

He was silent. Then, "Why archery?"

"Why not archery?"

45

"Fine, but no to the ocean."

"Why no to the ocean?"

"It's dangerous," he said, sipping the wine. Every time he tipped the goblet, Psyche expected wine to spill out but it never did.

"It's not as if I'm going to jump in," she said, feeling irritated.

"I never said you were. But there are things lurking in their depths that would make you suffer even if you kept to the shore."

That sobered her up, though it didn't completely rid her of her curiosity. "What kind of creatures?"

"Are you sure you want to know?"

"Do your worst," she said.

And so he spent the night telling her of all the terrible monsters that inhabited the ocean. At some point, Psyche fell asleep and by the time she woke up, he was gone.

XV Upwards

"Artemis and Athena are pushing upwards," Anteros said.

Eros shot a dozen of arrows into a man whose legs have been cut off.

They were in the middle of a battlefield and upwards meant closer to Psyche's kingdom.

Screams steeped the air.

This one had been a particularly cruel confrontation. Men and women on both sides had been maimed or killed. Eros wondered if he was making a mistake, helping Ares. His doubt became more apparent when he saw innards spilling out of men and horses. He remembered telling Psyche about the bloodthirsty monsters that inhabited Poseidon's realm and wondered how different he was from them.

An arrow, a human made one, grazed Eros's upper arm as he considered the carnage around. The lull in the fighting was seizing as new forces replaced the old. Eros hissed as Anteros raised his shield higher to protect them from a new onslaught of arrows.

There were different kinds of chaos and Eros found he didn't enjoy this kind very much. But he fought anyway. He had to fight so he could stop them from reaching Psyche's home. He had to fight like the monster he was.

And at the end of the battle, Apollo was on the losing side.

XVI A Monster with Wings

As another week passed, her host came every day. Each time he brought her new books and told her tales of the world. Sometimes they walked along the gardens, sometimes they flew over the island, and sometimes they just sat at the table, each reading a book of their choosing. Though he was far quicker at finishing those books than her. But then, he got another message and disappeared for two weeks.

Two weeks felt like an eternity.

Psyche had a target put up in the room and she was practicing archery when suddenly she felt someone behind her. Invisible hands brushed over her back, fixing her posture, and righting her grip. Her pulse turned erratic, thundering in her ears.

"Like this," the familiar voice said. She'd thought about him a lot in the time he was gone. She wondered who he was and wondered why she was beginning to grow fond of his visits. Began to long for them even.

"You smell of smoke," she said, releasing the arrow. It hit the heart of the target.

"You're quite good," he said, still standing behind her, his arms on her.

"You're changing the subject."

"The smoke is nothing," he said as he gave her another arrow and she fired it, "but you've made great process."

"I used to watch the captain of the guard a lot."

His grip tensed. "And he was good?"

"Very."

Tired laughter rumbled through him, though she could feel the tension underneath. "You were always very curious then?"

"I'd probably put Pandora to shame."

"Hmm," he said. "Probably."

Psyche turned to face him. His hands slid down to her waist. "You sound tired."

"I am."

She nodded at the bed. "Go sleep then."

"And you?"

"I still need to finish my practice and read."

"And how's reading?"

Psyche pursed her lips. "Great. I never imagined learning about Hades would be as fun as it was."

"You can't see it," he said, "but I'm smiling. I haven't smiled in a while."

She raised an eyebrow. "Is it because I look funny?" She knew her hair was a knot-ridden mess. "My hair?"

"No," he said, the smile still in his voice. He touched a strand of her hair. "Not at all." His hand lingered there and then moved down to her cheek.

Psyche's froze, breathless. She had expected this, wanted it sometimes, but now that it was real, she didn't know how to be. She just felt awkward and terrified. Heat neared her face as he leaned in close. The empty room didn't feel so empty anymore. She felt warm all over and not just from the practice of archery.

Then he laughed as if he couldn't quite believe what he was doing.

Psyche's mouth was dry so she didn't even attempt to speak for fear of jumbling her words but she did frown. *Was he judging her?*

"I'm sorry." His fingers trailed down to her neck and his thumb touched her bottom lip. "I'm being rather brazen."

Psyche still said nothing. *What was there to say? Yes, you are, but I don't mind?*

Then he pulled her closer, tightening his hold on her waist, no sign of real regret. She could feel the humanness of him, the warmth, and she was extremely thankful for the bow she was still gripping to her chest, which allowed for some distance between them.

Psyche swallowed as something touched her neck. She realized it was his lips.

She flinched and he froze. Slowly, she felt him rest his forehead on her shoulder. "I shouldn't have. I'm sorry."

Psyche cleared her throat. Although she was burning with an unexplainable desire to be held by him, she knew it was inappropriate. They were not actually wed. So, she just patted his head, feeling soft curls. He leaned into her touch for a moment and, with a deep sigh, moved away. She heard the bed creak as he lied down.

After a little bit his breathing evened out, so Psyched put the bow away and lied down beside him.

Psyche woke up to feather light touches on her face.

Then she felt a warm body tangled between her arms and legs. At first, she thought she was back home, sleeping with Elara. Her sister always complained about Psyche's propensity to hug anything in her sleep. But then Psyche remembered that her host had come last night and that *he* was the one lying in bed with her, not her sister.

Psyche's eyes snapped open only to find an empty bed and her own extremities floating in odd positions.

Am I going crazy?

But no, she could feel the sleeping body beneath and the feathers on her face. For they *were* feathers, as soft and living as the wings of a bird. Which led her to the question, what kind of a man had wings on his back? None. And Psyche could only think of a few gods: Hermes, Eros, Hypnos, Thanatos, but they couldn't be real, not in the way she was real. Could they? But as she reached out to feel the feathers with her hands, she found nothing but air. No feathers, no wings.

Psyche blinked, wondering if she was still asleep.

Without waking him, she moved her arm and sat up. That's when she noticed the blood on his side of the bed. It was fresh. He must have had an open wound.

"Bring bandages here," she whispered to the servants. "And breakfast."

They brought up bandages and ointments followed by trays of breads and figs and a jug of wine. It was the sounds of clattering dishes that awoke him before she could. She knew because he made the noises a waking person made as they stretched and came to.

"Good morning," she said.

"Morning."

"You're hurt," she said, pointing to the bandages between them. "Use these."

"I'll be fine," he said.

Psyche raised her bloody hand. "This doesn't look fine."

"An old wound must have opened up."

"Why?"

He breathed out through his nose.

"Tell me what's going on."

"I don't know if you want to know," he said.

"I wouldn't be asking you if I didn't want to know."

"Alright." He sighed. "There isn't an easy way to say this."

"So just say it."

"There's a war."

Psyche's heart sank as the Oracle's words came back to her. "What?"

The gods will forsake your kingdom in times most difficult.

What if this war was what the Oracle meant? "Where?"

"It started in Corinth."

"And now?"

"A lot of city-states and kingdoms are falling prey to it."

"What," she started. "What about my kingdom?"

"It'll reach it in a week's time."

Psyche couldn't deny the truth. She had refused to marry him and now her kingdom would pay the price. She couldn't have that. "You must marry me," she said, her voice quiet.

Silence. Then. "What?"

She turned to him or rather in his general direction. "Marry me or else the gods will forsake my kingdom."

"What are you talking about?"

"Apollo's prophecy," Psyche said, remembering that day in Delphi. The laughter. "It said I am to wed you, but we are *not* wed. And I don't want harm to come to my kingdom because of me."

"The war would have come anyway, marriage or no marriage. But I promise you this, the gods won't forsake your kingdom."

Psyche looked down at her hands. "You don't know that."

"I do."

"How would you?"

"I just do."

Psyche shook her head. "We *must* marry. We're living together anyhow. It won't be any different."

There was a long, long pause.

"Unless," Psyche narrowed her eyes. "Unless I'm not to your liking anymore?"

At that he choked and then laughed it off. "You… I promise your kingdom won't be forsaken, marriage or no marriage, do you hear."

"And what about my sisters," she said. "Will they be safe?" The palace would be protected by many guards and there'd be secret passageways for her *yiayia* and mother to get away, but her sisters didn't live in palaces.

Their homes would be raided, burnt down. They would be used and killed.

There was silence.

"Can you bring them here?"

"I—"

"Please," she pleaded, searching for his hand. "Please, bring them here."

A warm, big hand covered hers. "Alright."

Psyche nodded. As he began to pull his hand back, she held on to it. "And please, be safe yourself."

His quiet laughter was dark and self-deprecating. "I'm not anybody for you to worry about."

"Maybe you're not, maybe you are," she said.

"I was thinking," he said. "Once the war is over, and it *will* be over, you can return home with your sisters."

"But the prophecy. What if there is another war? Another disaster?"

"Apollos' prophecies rarely mean what you think."

Psyche swallowed, trying to make sense of everything he'd said, trying to believe him despite the fear and worry setting in.

He squeezed her hand. "I'll bring your sisters here tonight. Everything will be well."

She smiled.

After that, he left, leaving only bloodstains, bandages, and uncertainty behind.

XVII Disappear Into Forever

Zephyrus helped Eros find Psyche's sisters and carry them to the palace.

Their husbands had gone off to fight in the war, so convincing her sisters to come with him wasn't difficult. It was their servants that presented a challenge for his newly acquired conscience. Eros told them to go east, where the war wouldn't reach but he couldn't do much else. He wasn't the god of fortune, so he could only hope they listened to a bodiless voice.

When he'd promised Psyche that the gods wouldn't forsake her kingdom, he meant it. He would do everything in his power to keep it safe.

When Eros and Zephyrus arrived at the palace, it was night. All the lights in the palace were burning, so the whole place glimmered and danced like a fire. Psyche waited on the balcony. Eros's heart started beating faster.

Who would've thought that the god of desire would be trembling like a leaf at the sight of a mortal girl?

And the kiss? He could hardly believe how much he'd been shaking then, like a foolish mortal adolescent. It was rather embarrassing really but he really couldn't help himself.

He landed with the younger sister in his hands and put her down. Zephyrus set down the eldest one. And Psyche rushed to them, the worry in her eyes turning to joy.

"Oh," she exclaimed. "Oh, you're here."

They hugged and stayed locked in that embrace for a while.

Zephyrus nodded to Eros and disappeared into the night.

To give them privacy, Eros strolled out into the halls. The cherubs who had this week's shift greeted him. He greeted them back.

When he was near one of the gardens, a cherub came to him, his curls catching the glint of firelight. "Psyche is asking if you're still in the palace. What should I tell her?"

Eros hid his shaking hands. "Tell her to meet me by the lake."

The cherub inclined his head and flew away.

Eros headed out towards the water, thinking of everything he wanted to say to her but couldn't. He didn't regret promising to let her go after the war. Not yet. He felt that it was the right decision, at least for her. Even if it tore him apart, all he wanted was for her to be happy. And with him, she didn't have that chance.

Eros passed through a path guarded by hyacinths and carnations to the lake that glimmered with the light of a thousand stars. Night birds sang their songs along with crickets and whispering bushes.

It was peaceful here, peaceful enough to make him forget about the rest of the world burning.

Footsteps broke him out of his reverie.

"Hello," Psyche called out. "Are you out here?"

Eros took a deep breath. "Yes."

"Where exactly?"

With his sandaled feet, Eros made an X on the bank. "Here."

She came to stand beside him, her *peplos* rippling in the breeze. She was radiant. He realized he'd never truly seen her happy and now that he has, he would never be able to bear her sadness.

"I wanted to thank you," she said.

"Of course, it's the least I can do."

"The Oracle may have said you're a monster, but I don't believe it," Psyche went on.

When she said it, Eros wanted it to be true.

She reached out with her hands and found his face. Her fingers were marble cold against him and gentle as dawn. "I think you're wonderful."

And maybe he shouldn't have, maybe he would regret it, but in that moment all Eros could do was pull her to him without that damned bow between them and feel her warmth. He never wanted to let her go. She felt so nice in his arms. In that moment, he didn't know how he could have lived his *entire* life without her. How he could live it once she was gone.

Pain erupted in his chest at that thought. He winced.

"Is everything alright?" Psyche asked.

He straightened without letting her go. "Now it is." Then he did the only thing he could do. He leaned down and kissed her. The world seemed to disappear when their lips touched, and Eros wanted nothing more than to kiss her until he too disappeared.

Just this one memory. He could allow himself just this one memory.

She gasped as she tried to breathe and it was all he could do to break the kiss.

Eros watched Psyche as she caught her breath. The blue moonlight bathed her features and he wondered how he could have ever thought her less than perfect.

"I have never seen you," she said. "I don't even know your name. So why do I feel like we've met before? Like I've known you all my life."

Eros's breathing tightened. "I don't know."

"Can Eros make people fall in love with those whom they can't see?"

Eros tried not to react to his name. "I'm sure he's done worse."

Psyche smiled as if she knew. "You're right."

Eros froze, wondering if he should tell her. He wanted to, he wanted to so badly, but their love would lead nowhere. She was a mortal. He was not.

He forced himself to step away from her.

This had to be enough for him.

"I, uh, sorry," Psyche said.

Eros was very sensitive to her moods and he could feel her disappointment at the distance he'd put between them. He ached to close it again but that would only prolong his pain. Even if she wanted to be with him, the gods would never let it be. His mother would never let it be. They were petty. They would find ways to torture her or else use him against her before she even came close to earning her immortality. And he couldn't let her suffer at their whims.

"I just wanted to thank you," she said. "For bringing them to me."

He nodded, forgetting she couldn't see. "You're welcome."

"Are you going to leave again?"

"Yes."

Her face looked stricken. "How long will you be gone this time?"

"I don't know," he said.

She nodded, almost to herself. "If you need help, you know where to find me."

"I do."

XVIII Oil Lamps and the End of the World

The following few weeks, Psyche showed her sisters around the grounds. They found new rooms with musical instruments and towers with breathtaking views. Elara discovered a room full of statues, while Leda found another garden, this one with a drove of butterflies.

Psyche was almost the happiest she'd ever been. The only stain in her joy was the absences of the rest of her family and her nameless host, friend, first kiss. She didn't know how to think of him. But she knew that if she had an eternity with those people, Psyche would have been the most fortunate person on earth.

She looked at Elara, who was clutching her stomach from laughter at something Leda had said. They looked so content, sitting on a bedspread on grass.

"More water please," Psyche said.

"I almost feel like we're goddesses," Elara said. "With invisible servants."

Leda sighed. "Who'd have thought such wonders existed."

"I wish *yiayia* was here," Elara said.

"Me too," Psyche said. "I hope she's safe."

And there it was, a crack in their happiness. The mere thought of war soured everything.

"Could you ask the host to find out where she is?" Leda asked.

"I'll try, *if* he shows up."

Elara pulled her hair back.

"So you've never seen him then," Leda said.

Psyche shook her head.

"I hope he's Hermes," Elara said. They've looked through many books, scouring for who might be Psyche's mysterious friend and still couldn't figure it out.

"I hope he's Eros," Leda said.

Psyche put her head on Leda's lap. "Which of them is the nicer one?"

"They're gods," Elara said, "nice isn't one of the qualities they're known for."

Psyche made a face.

"You know," Leda started, playing with Psyche's hair, "I was thinking of something."

"I knew it," Elara said. "I knew it." She'd told Psyche many times that Leda was somewhat distracted, though they blamed it on worry for her husband. "You're hiding something."

"Not exactly hiding…"

"Spit it out," Psyche said.

"A few months ago, a strange old man gave me an oil lamp in the marketplace," Leda said. "He told me that it would shed light on things unseen. I didn't think much of it then, just some drivel, but it was free, so I took it. And… don't you think it was fate?"

Psyche looked up at her older sister's face. Her brows were knitted over her eyes as she thought of the lamp.

"You should've told us sooner," Elara said.

"I thought about it but then I didn't want to put Psyche in danger. What if she used the lamp and the host got mad?"

"So why are you telling us now?" Psyche asked.

"Because anyone who can create this much beauty," she answered, looking at the swaying blades of grass and flowering trees, "cannot be too cruel."

"Wait," Elara said, "so you have the lamp here?"

Leda nodded.

Psyche felt a thrill course through her. She'd been curious about what he looked like since the first time she'd heard him talk. And she knew that if he was going to let her leave with her sisters when the war ended, she'd never get to see him. That fear had irked her and now the gods were giving her an opportunity.

Is it worth betraying him?

Psyche frowned.

Does it count as betraying him?

"I need to think about it," Psyche said.

She thought about it all day and in the end, she couldn't help but give into her curiosity.

That evening, she went to Leda's room and asked for the lamp.

Leda rummaged through her basket. Ever the thoughtful one, she had filled it with food and spare clothes before being taken here.

"Here," she said, taking out an old oil lamp with a sun painted on cracked green paint.

For three more nights Psyche looked at it before going to bed. Could curiosity really ruin her?

On the third night, she felt him get into the bed beside her quietly when he thought she was sleeping. He must have been more tired than usual because he collapsed and fell asleep right away.

One peek wouldn't hurt.

Then when he kissed her again, she would know who to imagine.

Quietly, Psyche got out of bed and got the lamp.

It might not even work, she told herself.

She brought a piece of rolled up parchment paper to a low burning fire in one of the torches and used that flame to light the lamp. It came to life with a strange, quivering vigor. The light it gave off was the yellow gold of the sun, not of a fire, and it seemed to be pulling the darkness into it.

Psyche held it close to her body and thought for another minute.

Then with a quiet resolution, she turned and brought it to the empty bed. But now, the bed was no longer empty. Wherever the light touched, she saw what she hadn't been able to see before. Or rather who.

Her host turned out to be the most exquisite young man she'd ever seen. He had the face of a god and hair more golden than the brightest gold. He stretched languorously on the bed, his muscles only partially covered with the covers.

Despite herself, Psyche brought it closer.

She couldn't get enough of his face. The long eyelashes, the perfect angles.

There was no mistaking his like. It was Eros in all his glory.

Psyche didn't understand. Couldn't understand, why someone like Eros would ever even think of someone like her. And as she thought, a drop of burning oil dripped on the god's arm and he woke up.

Their eyes met, his were the clearest blue. A jolt went through Psyche.

Then Eros's bewildered expression twisted into that of agony and he cried out in pain.

Psyche tried to put out the lamp, but it wouldn't go out, only burn her. She even tried to pour the oil out, but it didn't budge. The shadows continue piling into it. So, she tossed it across the room and went over to Eros, who began to shake and tremble as light went out of him and became shadow before being pulled into the lamp.

"What," he got out. Then he looked utterly confused. "Psyche?"

"I," Psyche shook her head, horrified at what she'd done. She never blamed herself for her curiosity. It was always the thing that gave her a sense of power, a sense of freedom, a sense of autonomy over her life. It had always been her blessing. But now, now it felt like a curse.

Eros opened his wings and stood up, though convulsions still racked his body.

"Don't go," she said. "Please."

"We can't stay here," he managed. "It's not safe."

"I'm sorry. I just wanted to see you."

He went to the window and called out to Zephyrus. To Psyche he said, "Get your sisters, go outside, Zephyrus will take you away from here."

"What about you?"

Eros clothed his eyes in pain. "Goodbye, Psyche." Then he jumped. Psyche could only watch his form disappear into the distance.

Not long after, the palace began to move. It began with a crack beneath her feet. Then the floor began coming apart. Ceilings caved in.

A little cherub appeared next to Psyche. It didn't take her long to realize that they had been her servants.

"What have you done?" he said, his eyes filled with betrayal and hatred.

Others joined in blaming her.

That's when Leda and Elara burst into her room and swatted the cherubs away from Psyche.

"We have to get out of here," Leda said.

The cherubs flew away, one by one.

Psyche and her sisters ran outside as the palace began to fall apart around them. It was louder than thunder. An apocalypse.

"Where now?" Elara asked.

"We're on an island," Psyche said.

And as if it heard her, the island itself began to quake. A crack opened beneath their feet. So, they held hands and together ran towards the shore.

Leda fell along the way, twisting her ankle. "Go," she said.

"You're an idiot," Elara said. "In what world would we leave you behind?"

And so, Psyche and Elara lifted her up and carried her onwards, tripping on the hems of their *peplos*.

Somewhere along the way, the wind caught them, and they were flying. It took them higher and higher and from there Psyche could see the island go underwater and disappear as if it had never been.

Psyche's heart sank with it.

The flight lasted for a small eternity but soon they were on a familiar shore.

"Please," Psyche said. "Don't go yet. Tell me where I can find Eros."

The wind circled her once and then a strong gust of it roared around them.

"Hey, watch it," Elara shouted, running over to Psyche.

"Please," Psyche said, looking to Zephyrus, "please. I meant no harm."

This was Eros's last kindness to you, the wind replied. *Now he is forever out of your reach. Forget him.*

And he too was gone.

XIX Agonizing Betrayal

Shattering pain reverberated through Eros as if he was a hollow statue. It threatened to send him to Tartarus and melt his very being for all of eternity.

Eros didn't know how he'd reached his abode. If he had reached it at all. But at some point, when the pain subsided for a fraction of a second, he saw clouds around him. Familiar, magnificent clouds. Then a new wave of pain crashed over his judgement and reeled him back into torture.

The worst of it all, the *very worst* of it, was that this had been done through Psyche. Which meant the gods knew. The gods knew and who knows what would befall her now. And he, Eros, could do nothing.

"Eros," his brother's voice came.

Anteros.

Eros thought he'd said the name out loud but then realized he could not speak.

Please, help her. He thought. *Anteros, help her.*

But then darkness claimed Eros to the sound of mocking laughter.

XX Anteros, a Crowd of Cupids, and a Question

Anteros watched the godly glow drain from his brother. One wouldn't know it was there until it wasn't and only a grey shell of who he was remained.

Eros wasn't dead; it took much more than a cursed poison to kill a god. Still, Eros was weak.

Anteros kneeled next to him and brushed his matted hair back.

A crowd of his brother's cherubs burst in through the clouds, not even creating a door before they did.

"It was Psyche and her sisters," one of the cherubs cried. And then the rest burst into unintelligible drivel. Their small voices filled the grand abode, filled Anteros's head to a pounding headache.

"Enough," he shouted. His voice echoed with authority.

The cherubs stopped.

"One of you," he said, pointing at the one who had begun to speak, "please, explain."

The little one fluttered its wings and flew closer. "Psyche's sisters gave her an oil lamp that would let her see our master. And she, having been born of Pandora, let her curiosity get the best of her. The light took all the shadows and when a drop of oil touched the master, he began to scream."

A light that swallowed shadows?

That didn't sound like a simple cursed poison.

"Did they know it was poisoned?" Anteros asked because if they did, he would reckon with them. Betrayal was an unforgivable sin.

"No, I don't think—" the first one began to say but others interrupted him.

"We don't know."

Anteros looked at his brother. It was odd seeing him lifeless, odd to see his abode in such dull colors.

"Alright," he said, raising his voice once again to quiet the clamor. "Watch him. I need to figure out what this curse is before it's too late."

XXI Two Sides of a Coin

Elara led the way home through a smoky dawn and awakening villages.

True to his word, Eros had managed to protect most of their kingdom, though, if rumors were to be believed, the far reaches of it were razed to the ground. The far reaches where Leda had lived.

Leda winced with every step.

Psyche held her upright. And that was the only thing that kept Psyche herself from falling apart.

"I'm sorry," Leda said.

"It's not your fault," Psyche replied.

"No, it is. If I hadn't told you about that lamp. If I had just kept it to myself."

"Please…"

"I had a bad feeling about it and still."

"Leda," Psyche said, slowing down. Elara trekked farther down the dusty road, acting as a lookout. "I don't blame you."

"But you blame yourself. And I'm telling you, it wasn't your fault."

Psyche looked down at the small pebbles beneath their feet. "My curiosity has always gotten me in trouble."

"There are two sides to that coin," Leda said. "Remember how many times it's gotten you out of trouble? Or brought us joy?"

Psyche looked up at her sister.

Leda smiled. "Now me, I was always a little envious of you. What if I gave it to you because I knew it'd hurt you?"

Psyche raised an eyebrow.

"It's true." Leda sighed. "You were always praised for your beauty and I… well, I was just the first daughter, to be married off undiscerningly, so you and Elara could find husbands."

"Hey," Elara shouted. "Are you two coming?"

Psyche hugged her sister, still holding her up. "I'm sorry."

Leda sniffled and then laughed at herself. "I'm being pathetic. Again."

"I'll tell you who was pathetic," Psyche said. "Your husband was. And father. You deserved much better. You still do."

"Thank you," Leda said. "You do too."

Elara came running down the road. "Are you saying bad things behind my back?" she asked, out of breath.

"The most terrible things," Leda said.

And Psyche drew Elara into their hug.

"But really," Elara said, "I don't like secrets."

"We were talking about how Psyche needs to go after Eros and find us god husbands as well," Leda said.

Elara burst out laughing.

Psyche looked at Leda, wondering if she was serious.

Leda nodded.

A plan was already forming in Psyche's mind.

"Wait, you're not laughing," Elara said, glancing from one sister to another. "And I feel stupid. Stop leaving me out."

"I'm going to Eros's temple," Psyche said. "I'm going to try to talk to him."

"I don't know if you've noticed but he seemed pretty angry, at least judging by the cupids. Those babies looked about ready to claw your eyes out."

"I have to try," Psyche said.

"You can't go alone," Elara said.

"Leda needs rest, and you need to help her."

"Then wait. There's still a war raging on."

But Psyche had already decided. "The time is now."

"But you'll be alone," Elara said, getting desperate. "The three of us got such dirty looks. What will you do by yourself? What will you do if bad people come at you?"

"I don't know," Psyche said, squeezing Elara's hand.

They stood quietly on the road, each with questions and dreams and worries of their own, but each connected with an unbreakable thread.

Then Elara broke the silence, pulling a small pouch of coins from a hidden pocket in her dress. "Take these."

"Your stash," Psyche said.

Elara put it in her palm. "Return and pay me back."

Psyche nodded.

When they reached a crossroads, her sisters went one way and Psyche another.

XXII Abandoned by the Gods

It was a tricky business being a lone girl on the road, so the first order of business was to buy a concealing cloak.

Eros's temple was a long walk away, in the city of Artosa on the edge of the kingdom. If Psyche hoped to get there whole, she needed to blend in and blend in well.

At the first village she came upon, she went to the market. It was a small place and so people ogled her with grim expressions. Psyche had to move fast before she invited trouble. She found a couple of stalls that sold cloaks but when she stopped to buy one, the men refused to talk to her. Nor would they accept her money. Finally, she found a meager stall at the end of the market. It only held a few items and the man behind it looked as if he hadn't eaten well in weeks.

He squinted at her but didn't speak, no doubt waiting for her chaperone.

"I want to buy this cloak," Psyche said.

He still said nothing.

She tossed a silver coin on the fabrics he'd spread as displays.

He frowned as he took the coin. It was far more than the cloak cost. He bit the coin, though he only had two good teeth. When he was sure it was not a fake, he waved at the cloak unceremoniously.

"Thank you," Psyche said and as she took the cloak, she slid another coin to him.

His eyebrows rose and his lip began to quiver, even as he refused to let it.

Psyche inclined her head and left.

The merchant wasn't the last poor and destitute person Psyche saw during her travels. And the number of them increased as she neared the border. There were people who lost their homes, people who lost loved ones. Refugees came to this kingdom, having been thrown out of their own kingdoms. They all gathered in dark corners or abandoned temples, trying to make their world make sense again, trying to piece back the bits of their lives. But work was scarce, as was food.

Psyche had to always be alert, sleeping only a few hours at a time.

It got worse, when she reached the villages that have been ruined. People with dead eyes sat in rubbles or moaned over makeshift graves. Remnants of life meekly coursed through here.

Psyche bought apples and bread and she had olives she'd taken from someone's abandoned garden. She stopped near the unfortunate with haunted eyes and offered them food. She remembered the first man she'd stopped by. His face was dirty, and flies circled him, even though it was cold outside. Slowly, he blinked up at her. And took the apple. Then the bread. His hands were as good as skeletons.

There were many like him.

For weeks, Psyche saw the wreckage of life after a war. Her heart bled for the suffering. And she couldn't help but wonder if Eros had been responsible for some of the damage. Maybe not here, in her kingdom, but other places.

When nights got unbearably cold, Psyche joined refugees in abandoned temples.

One time, she found a small temple honoring Demeter. Although much of it was destroyed, she knew it was hers by wheat stalks and stylized poppy flowers engraved on the frieze.

Psyche went inside and was met by a foul odor she had come to associate with the dead. There were so many dead people on the road.

In the hearth, she found a low fire still burning, so she brought it to life by blowing on it gently and adding wood. Once it was bright enough to illuminate the temple,

Psyche saw three corpses sprawled on the floor. One was still in the position of worship.

Psyche looked away, the apple she'd eaten in the morning threatening to come back out.

Once she steeled herself, Psyche walked over to the body closest to her and grabbed the cold hands. With great effort, she dragged it out to the back. The temple had a burnt down garden. She lined up the bodies in the garden and made a pyre. She put coins on each of their eyes. Then burnt them, so they could have peace in the afterlife.

Her hands were numb by the time the bodies were gone and the fire put out.

Before going to sleep, Psyche cleaned up the temple, picking up torches and wiping the dirt with her cloak. In the corner, she found a small statue of Demeter knocked over to its side. It was heavy, heavier than the bodies, so it took Psyche a lot of effort to get it back up. As she did, she kept getting poked by her crown of flowers. But with persistence and a sturdy branch, Psyche stood her up. Then, with a small prayer to the goddess, she fell asleep.

The next day, she was on the road again. Her limbs were screaming but she made herself march forward. She couldn't stop, not yet.

Towards evening, Psyche heard voices. When she looked over her shoulder, she saw a group of men at the top of a hill. These men didn't look destitute. They looked like barbarians. And they were pointing at her.

An easy prey.

Psyche's blood ran cold.

Run, she told herself. *Run.*

Her mind reeled and sputtered, but then her body moved, and she was running faster than she'd ever run in her life.

Her feet were raw from her long journey. Her mind was exhausted. But Psyche pushed herself with all she had because she knew that if these men caught her, she would be as good as dead. Worse than dead. And she didn't make it this far only to have everything ruined by them.

However, the gods must have really cursed Psyche, because one of the men did catch up with her. And tackled her to the ground.

XXIII A Favor Returned

Pain reverberated through Psyche's skull and stars swam behind her eyes.

"You dare run, boy?" the man growled. But when he turned her around, he saw that she wasn't a boy at all. "Look at who we have here." He hooted as he called his friends. "We got ourselves a bit of fun."

They joined him and laughed when they saw him straddling her with his heavy weight.

"A pretty maiden," another said. "I haven't seen such pretty maidens before."

Psyche struggled against him but in vain.

The man leaned over her, pulling her dress up. "Squirmy wench."

"Let me go," Psyche screamed. She kicked out and aimed for his face. But then the others grabbed her arms and pinned them down.

"Don't break her," someone said. "You're not the only one here."

The man laughed.

Disgusting.

Psyche closed her eyes, hating her own helplessness and waited for the worst. But the worst never came. Instead, they screamed, and the weight of the man disappeared.

When Psyche opened her eyes, she saw all five of them enclosed in small hurricanes of dust. They grabbed at their throats and closed their eyes, but the dust got inside them, choking them. Then, as suddenly as it'd started, the hurricanes stopped, and the men fell to the ground. They didn't move.

Psyche pushed her skirts down with trembling hands.

A beautiful woman walked out with a crown of flowers upon her head and a flowing *peplos* of deep greens and warm browns. She looked like Demeter.

"My child," the goddess said with a voice that filled Psyche with healing warmth. She reached out and helped Psyche get up.

"Demeter?" Psyche asked.

"Indeed."

Tears spilled down Psyche's cheeks at the sight of her warm smile. It was like being with a mother. Psyche missed her mother and her *yiayia*.

Demeter let her cry.

Psyche cried and cried, letting all the fear and frustration pour out of her. Then she wiped the tears with the back of her hand and looked at the goddess.

"I know who you are," Demeter said. "And I know what you want."

"I didn't mean to hurt him," Psyche said. "I just want to talk to him, to explain."

"He's not well," Demeter said. "But I can't take you to him."

"Not well? But he's a god."

Demeter smiled sadly. "Gods have their own rules of living too."

"It wasn't just an oil lamp, was it?"

"There's a war, as you're well aware of and the gods have split. To win, each side will do terrible things to the other," Demeter said. "The oil lamp was just one method of weakening the side Eros was on. "

"Is there anything I can do?" Psyche asked.

"Go to Aphrodite's temple," Demeter said. "And plead with her."

Then the goddess patted Psyche's head, making a small flower wreath appear on top of it. "This will protect you and help you in time of need."

75

XXIV The Begetting of the Tasks

Anteros was by Aphrodite's side when the mortal girl called on her.

"Shall I skin her alive?" the goddess said, seething. "Or make her die of thirst and hunger?"

Aphrodite's palace was an extravagant concoction of gilded clouds and columns made of ocean water in which fish with brilliant scales swam freely. She sat on her golden throne studded with precious rocks and had four dozen small gods and goddesses attending to her. Though her thoughts were far darker than everything else suggested.

"Don't be hasty," Anteros said.

"It wasn't enough that she stole away my followers but then she stole away my son. And now, because of her, Apollo got to Eros."

"I know."

"And he might seize to be a god."

"I know."

"Killing her wouldn't be enough," Aphrodite said. "But you can't. We need her."

"We can find someone else to go in her stead."

Anteros shook his head. "The cure has to be retrieved by one who administered it." Such was the rule of the poison Apollo had sent to Eros. And it was probably the only reason Aphrodite hadn't tortured Psyche to death yet.

Aphrodite let out an indignant breath. "Rules may be rules but I want vengeance. I want justice. I want her crawling on her knees and screaming until her throat bleeds."

Anteros understood his mother's sentiments, though he didn't agree with them. And he didn't think it was fair to blame mortals for their shortcomings. After all, the gods had plenty of those themselves. "Then test her."

Aphrodite gave him a look as if he was stupid. "What is she, Hercules? I said vengeance."

"Come up with tasks that accomplish both. Without killing her. Obviously."

"Don't talk to me that way. This was your fault too. You're fortunate I've been worn out by the war or you would be crawling out there with that mortal worm."

Anteros rolled his eyes.

"As for the tasks," Aphrodite said, a cruel smile spreading across her lips. "I think I've just thought of a few."

XXV The Seeds

Psyche knelt in front of Aphrodite's golden statue until the sun went down.

"Please," she said again. "Please."

"Dirty, pathetic human how dare you sleep in my temple," a haughty voice boomed, coming from everywhere at once.

Psyche shot up to her feet only to find herself in a cage made of enormous fingers.

"And what a stench you bring," the voice said, lifting Psyche up by her hair. "What did anyone ever find in you?"

The pain was almost unbearable, but Psyche refused to scream in the face of a goddess. A giant face. Beautiful but so inhuman as to be frightening. Her eyes were volatile oceans, her lips, bloody stretches of velvet, her hair, tapestries of gold. There was no doubt about who it was. Aphrodite.

"I've come to talk to Eros," Psyche gritted out, overcoming her sheer shock and ignoring the pain in her scalp.

Aphrodite laughed. Psyche was getting used to the cruel laughter of the gods. "And who says I will let you?"

"I want him to know I meant no harm. I was beginning to like him too much and I—"

"Enough," Aphrodite said, flinging Psyche to the ground.

The impact was instant and thunderous, snapping her left wrist in half. Marble was not the best thing to fall on. Not the best thing at all.

"Stand up," Aphrodite said.

Psyche pushed to her feet, feeling even more insignificant than before.

"I wanted to kill you as soon as I saw you," Aphrodite said, shoving Psyche back with a single finger.

"The insolent girl who not only stole my followers away but who enchanted my son."

Psyche fell, broken and bruised in front of the goddess.

"But I think killing you would be too easy."

To say Psyche wasn't afraid would be a lie. She was terrified. But she was also a little bit thrilled. A few months ago, she hadn't even known gods were real. She had faith, of course, but faith was different than actual evidence. And this, having been chosen by the gods, even as someone to torture, made Psyche feel like she was more than just a young girl waiting to marry whoever her parents chose.

"Rather," Aphrodite went on, "I'll give you three tasks. If you fulfill all of them, I will let you see Eros before you die."

Psyche dared to look up. "Could we, maybe come to a different arrangement?"

Aphrodite cocked her head, as if a piece of dirt had spoken.

"O Magnificent Aphrodite, the goddess more beautiful than all," Psyche added.

Aphrodite did not look flattered. "You'll be silent, or our arrangement will change to you being thrown into a lake of fire."

Psyche averted her gaze.

"Your first task," Aphrodite said, "is to separate all the seeds into different piles."

As she said those words, they were transported to an enormous hall piled to the ceiling with seeds.

Psyche had better odds surviving a lake of fire than separating all of the seeds in her lifetime. Though she didn't say that out loud.

"Get to it," Aphrodite said. She was a normal size now. "And do it on your knees."

Psyche said nothing.

Aphrodite disappeared.

79

As soon as she did, Psyche's whole body began to hurt with the bruises and cuts of her long journey. But her wrist hurt worst of all.

She lifted it into the air and watched it droop down like a boneless stalk.

"Who said adventures would be easy," Psyche said.

Trying to ignore the pain, Psyche glanced around. Hill upon hill of seeds and grains awaited her. She tried to move on her knees, but she couldn't get far without the seeds embedding themselves in her skin. Clearly, Aphrodite didn't want Psyche to succeed, which meant she merely wanted to see her suffer.

Psyche didn't have to pretend.

She hobbled around on her knees, trying to find an empty floor on which she could start the first pile. But the more she moved the seeds, the more of them avalanched down from the peaks of the hills. Her wrist was screaming, so she couldn't even walk on all fours. She slipped more than once in her attempts to see just how big the hall was.

Time flowed slower here. There was neither food, nor water. Psyche's eagerness sapped out little by little as her wrist swelled up. It felt like days passed and all she had to show for herself were three meager piles of barley, poppy seed, and chickpeas. They each came up to Psyche's shoulder but that was nothing compared to how much more there was left.

As Psyche was lying on a bed of seeds, delirious from pain, she remembered her flower wreath.

With a shaking hand, she took it and called on Demeter. "O Demeter, I hate to ask you another favor, but please help me once more."

A door of flowers appeared amidst the piles of seeds and Demeter stepped out. When she saw the piles of seeds, she whistled. "Aphrodite outdid herself," Demeter said. "But worry not, I will help you. You remind me of my daughter."

"Thank you," Psyche said.

In a moment it took Psyche to blink, all the seeds were separated. Even the ones that have been stuck to her were gone. And her crown with flowers withered.

Psyche almost cried in relief, but she didn't think crying twice in front of the same goddess was acceptable. "Thank you," she said.

Demeter smiled. "Good luck with your next task."

XXVI A Lucid Moment

Eros opened his eyes, fighting against the darkness and pain.

"Master," the cherubs cried.

"Eros," Anteros said, coming over to him. "How are you feeling?"

Words still escaped Eros. It was as if he'd broken an oath on Styx. He felt entirely vulnerable. And sad. Gods he felt sad.

"You were poisoned by Apollo but don't worry, we're going to get you the antidote soon," Anteros said. "I hope. It all depends on Psyche now."

Eros gave his brother a look. A questioning one.

"It's complicated. And now, Mother found out about Psyche and, well, it's all a mess but what else is new."

Eros recalled the night the poison touched him. He felt the island crash. *Psyche.* He wanted to ask Anteros about what happened to Psyche. About whether or not Zephyrus saved her.

"Don't worry, she's fine. For now."

Pain zigzagged through Eros's abdomen. His vision darkened.

So, it was Apollo's poison. He must have given it to one Psyche's sisters to get it to Psyche, knowing she'd be curious.

Eros sighed and the pain worsened.

When he got better, he'd show Apollo.

The pain burst like one of Zeus's bolts and the world turned to nothing.

"Just hold on," Anteros said. "Hold on."

XXVII Where Do the Forsaken Go?

Aphrodite examined the piles. "Clever, clever to use Demeter's help."

Psyche was still kneeling. A few of her scratches were infected. She was tired and parched for water.

"Now for the next task," Aphrodite began.

"O Aphrodite, will you be so kind as to allow me a drink first," Psyche said.

Aphrodite laughed. "Oh, you'll have plenty to drink, while you're filling this crystal flask with the black water of Styx."

Her voice echoed menacingly, and Psyche found herself standing on a cliff overlooking a river. There was fog surrounding it. It was night.

She looked up. No, it wasn't simply night. There were no stars in the sky, no clouds.

All sounds were gone.

She was in the Underworld, she realized. In the outer reaches of it, at least. The Styx winded like a snake and disappeared into the fog. To get to it, Psyche would have to climb down the face of the cliff. The only problem was that her wrist was still very much broken. Even the thought of it brought the ache pulsing back.

She hobbled along the cliff, finding no stairs or paths down. Despair began to take root in her heart.

There's nothing else to do but jump.

The thought startled Psyche.

It felt foreign in her mind.

Jump and you will reach Styx.

Psyche shook it away. She had read about the effects of the Underworld and it seemed to be getting to her now.

Think. There must be a way, she told herself.

83

There is no way, the voice hissed, slow and contemptuous.

Psyche swallowed.

You will die here.

And do you know what happens to the bodies of those mortals who die in the Underworld? Another voice joined in.

Psyche squinted at the river. A shape was coming nearer and nearer through the grey fog. The never-ending fog.

They don't decay. You will be trapped here for all of eternity.

A voice wailed in the distance.

That will be you. Crying for death, for torture, for anything.

But the gods will ignore you.

Where do the forsaken go?

Where do the forsaken go?

"Enough," Psyche said.

There used to be a girl and like all other mortals, she was forgotten.

The skin, the skull, and body rotten.

"No."

Yes, your cries were made for these walls.

Alone.

Forgotten.

Not alive.

Not dead.

Psyche covered up her ears because the voices were getting louder and louder.

Despair. So much despair. It filled her. It overwhelmed her. So much so that she began to scream. Scream as if the world was ending. Scream loudly and painfully. She screamed until her throat was hoarse. She screamed until tears came out of her eyes. She screamed even when she thought she couldn't anymore.

Stop.

Psyche wanted to stop. She was aware where she was, aware who she was, and yet she couldn't stop. The scream was unending.

She had to make it stop. To reach the river.

You'll never reach it.

Forever here.

No, she had to see her sisters, her family, and she had to see Eros.

With those thoughts in mind, Psyche stood up.

I have people I love.

I have people who love me.

Aphrodite, I thought you'd understand.

Then she ran towards the darkness that swathed the continuation of the cliff behind her. It was like falling into the ocean, but darker and colder.

Water was all around her.

Psyche choked on it, not having expected to find herself in water.

A sickly blue light shone on her from above and she swam. Her *peplos* and cloak got tangled in her feet but Psyche didn't let that stop her. She swam furiously and broke the surface with a loud gasp.

Her throat was raw, and she tasted blood. But when she looked up, she saw the cliff she had just been standing on, which meant she was in the Styx now.

Psyche paddled for the shore and once she reached it, she saw that the person in the fog was floating closer and closer.

Charon?

She had to act fast. With unsteady, but surprisingly unbroken hands, Psyche took out the flask and filled it.

The ominous figure was almost on the brink of the fog.

Psyche urged the water to fill faster. Almost. Almost.

85

When black liquid gurgled out of the mouth of the flask, Psyche jumped back from the water. The shadow left the fog but didn't appear beyond it. It was as if the shadow had been eaten by the fogless air.

Psyche shuddered.

Then a voice said, *Ready to take flight?*

Psyche jumped but then she recognized the wind, Zephyrus.

She nodded and he carried her out of the Underworld.

XXVIII Third Task

Zephyrus set her down outside of Aphrodite's temple.

That was brave of you, he said.

Psyche smiled with a small nod. Then her expression darkened. "Do you know how Eros is?"

Dying, was the reply.

Psyche shook her head, hit with a helpless sorrow. "He can't."

Zephyrus howled sadly and left.

Guilt washed over Psyche. Guilt and fear. She might not have loved Eros yet, but she didn't want to be the cause of his misery. Not after he did so much for her.

Psyche headed into the temple with the full resolve of telling Aphrodite about how she should be worried about Eros instead of playing useless games with mortals. But then she heard voices.

"She can do it," said a male voice. "We have to let her try."

"Yes, because she'll be so eager to go into the Underworld again." This was Aphrodite's voice.

"I'm sure she'll understand once we tell her it's for Eros."

"And what? You think Hades will simply hand the antidote over to her?"

"She passed your tests."

"Barely."

"Mother."

At that, Psyche opened the doors and went in. Aphrodite and a young man who looked like Eros but wasn't him, were having a conversation by the foot of her statue. It sounded so staged that Psyche almost thought they were thespians practicing their dialogue. But no, they were gods, and they were serious.

"I'll go," she said. "Is that my third task?"

Aphrodite gave her a look that could melt ice and then freeze it right after.

"Psyche," the young winged god said.

"You're not Eros," she said.

He inclined his head. "I'm his more cool-headed brother, Anteros."

"Nice to meet you."

"Ah, you have the water," he said, with a pointed look at Aphrodite. "Impressive."

"Give it to me," she said.

Anteros took the flask and handed it over to Aphrodite. She took it, unscrewed the cap, and tipped the flask. A stream of black water spilled out onto the temple floor.

Psyche said nothing. She kept all the indignance out of her face.

"Your third task is indeed to get an antidote for Eros," Aphrodite said, "since it must be retrieved by the person who administered the poison. But that doesn't mean I will spare you."

"She took a swim in the Styx, mother," Anteros said, "I'm sure she'll be a little difficult to kill now."

Aphrodite smiled. "Even better."

XXIX Crossing a River

Psyche no longer felt like the naïve girl she had been a few months ago. Indeed, she did not feel like herself at all. Even if war and Aphrodite hadn't been able to change her, standing at the gateway to Hell, waiting to enter the Underworld for the second time in one day, seemed to expand her mind and awareness in ways she could not have imagined.

As Anteros had said, the gateway was nothing special. It was a low congregation of rocks in the mountains. He had flown Psyche there but the rest was up to her. Though what exactly the rest was, Psyche didn't know. She supposed she had to find Hades.

Psyche took a step toward the gate and the view shimmered as if she'd passed some invisible point of no return. And then she was in a world different than the one she'd just been in. The landscape was still the same but now it was darker and inhabited by aimless shadows floating around above the mountains. Perhaps they were always there but now she could just see them.

During her stay at Eros's palace, Psyche had read about the Underworld. The book had said that outside of the entrance lived Grief, Diseases, and Fears. Just a little beyond, there was War and the domain of the dark-hearted gods like Erinyeas and Eris.

The shadows must have been Grief, Diseases, and Fears.

Psyche ducked as one flew over her head, trailing screams.

Before they could catch her, Psyche rushed to the rocks that made up the gate. It had a wooden door. She pulled it open to reveal a dark, small tunnel with a hellish light at the bottom.

Psyche hesitated.

Another shadow swooped over her, leaving her no other choice but to jump inside and shut the door behind her.

It was dark. A muffled scream sounded behind her as the shadow slammed against the door.

Psyche touched her heart and felt it beating through her ribcage. She went down before her courage could fail her. She told herself she was curious.

Step by step, she neared the light.

It opened up onto a big complicated cavern with all sorts of creatures prowling the packed dirt. In the midst of all of it, there stood an Elm tree with false dreams clinging to every leaf. Psyche put her hood over her head and kept close to the wall as she bypassed the chaotic thrum of unfamiliar life. Or was it non-life?

She remembered what the voices had said when she was on the cliff. *Not alive. Not dead.*

To clear out the echoes of pain, Psyche thought of Eros. Of his appearance, all she could remember were his blue eyes and golden curls. He looked like Aphrodite, with the same dreamlike expression and sensuous lips. He was beautiful. But more than that, she remembered how kind he was. How interesting.

And now he was dying.

Where would he go if he did die? Also, Hades? If they survived, Psyche would ask Eros about it.

She pressed through the throngs of centaurs and chimeras, finally reaching a tunnel that opened onto the Acheron River. Psyche stopped, watching naked people clamor towards a boat. Charon's boat.

They paid him their toll.

Since Psyche had dunked herself in the Styx, Anteros didn't think she'd need a toll, but she had extra gold coins anyway.

Psyche joined the crowd of the dead. They stared at her since she was very much clothed and very much alive.

Psyche did her best to keep her head straight and pointed at Charon. He was like a skeleton with a beard and a filthy cloak.

"No passage to the living," he said when her turn came about. His voice sounded ancient and unused.

"I have coins," Psyche replied.

"I said no passage to the living."

The dead pushed past her, shoving her aside. The ferry filled up, buoying on the black waters of Acheron. Two unlucky souls who haven't been buried were also stranded on the shore next to Psyche.

"Wait," Psyche called out.

"Do they not teach you anything above anymore?" Charon said. "In plain Greek, I'm telling you—"

"I know," Psyche said. "I just want to pay the toll for these two."

Charon's face scrunched up in distaste. She thought he'd say no again, but he stuck out his emaciated hand. She dropped the coins there and the two were permitted to board.

The ferry disappeared into the fog.

Now what?

XXX All Roads Lead to Hades

Psyche was never one to be completely out of outrageous ideas. Proof: what she was doing right now.

She took off her cloak and let if fall to the ground. She took a deep breath filled with the smell of damp earth and bones, then dipped her toe into the water.

For a river that was renowned as the river of pain, it didn't hurt. Psyche put her whole foot in, and still it washed over her skin like normal water.

"Well, here goes nothing," she said as she jumped.

She swam for a long time. The water got into her nose and mouth. It tasted salty but not like the ocean. This salt was reminiscent of tears and diseases. Psyche hoped it would give her neither.

Once she got to the other shore, she found another river to cross even though she had expected Hades's palace. Psyche stood not knowing what to do. She could swim it but how many more rivers would there be? Would she have to cross all six of the Underworld's rivers? What would that do to her?

She brushed her wet hair back and took a deep breath. It wasn't as if she had any choice. For Eros, she would do anything.

After a small eternity of swimming, she climbed ashore and froze because an enormous three-headed dog was coming her way and coming fast. Cerberus.

Psyche whimpered.

Cerberus roared and jumped at her. She fell in one fell swoop. Even a single paw was enough to crush her. And by all means she should have been crushed but something within her didn't give. She barely felt any pain at all. Then a loud whistle rang out through the cavern.

Cerberus jumped back.

"I'm so sorry for such a rude greeting," someone said. The voice was decidedly female and not at all afraid. "Cerberus doesn't like strangers."

When Cerberus got off Psyche and Psyche righted herself, she was met by an exquisite girl in the most elaborate *peplos* Psyche had ever seen. There was also a spread of flowers around her neck and woven through the dark curls that cascaded down her shoulders.

"I'm Persephone," the girl said.

Psyche nodded. "I'm Psyche."

"My mother told me you might come."

"I'm here for the remedy."

"Yes, for Eros," Persephone said, motioning to a grand door carved into the wall. "Take no offense, but I'm glad he finally got caught in his own trap."

"What do you mean?" Psyche asked.

"Oh, just that he'd given everyone hell…" she paused to shake her head at her choice of words, "with his arrows. And loudly pronounced on more than one occasion that he would never fall in love." Persephone laughed. "Fates are fair indeed."

Psyche frowned. "Eros had never been in love?"

"Not until you."

Psyche had hoped it was something along those lines even though she found it hard to believe.

The doors opened and they were in a whole other realm altogether. It was dark but not pitch black. An innumerable number of candles were melted into the walls. There were night flowers and butterflies and a mystical palace that floated in the middle of a depthless chasm. A breathtaking bridge stretched out from the end of the cliff they were on to the palace.

"It's beautiful," Psyche said.

Persephone laughed. "I know."

"So," Psyche started because if she didn't ask now, she'd never know, "can I ask you something… about you?"

"Did I come here of my own accord or was I kidnapped?" Persephone guessed.

"You get asked this a lot?"

Persephone continued to smile. "More than you'd imagine. But you will have to ask Eros that question."

"I'm afraid we're not going to be on speaking terms once he awakens."

"If he's still not talking to you after you save his life, I'll come up to the surface and murder him myself," Persephone said. She sounded completely serious. "Step carefully," she said once they reached the bridge.

Psyche watched the palace grow to an impossible height. The gates here were taller than anything she'd ever seen. Taller than a mountain.

"Gates of Hades," Persephone said. "I was impressed too."

Everything about the palace was impressive but if Psyche had to pick one thing, it would be Hades himself. He sat in his throne, pale hair flowing down a cloak of shadow. He was young and handsome, the picture of serenity and a harsh kind of splendor.

"Stop posing dear," Persephone said, joining him on the dais.

"I'm not," he replied.

"The girl has more pressing matters than your theatrics."

"Everyone loves my theatrics," he went on, cool and reserved.

Persephone sighed and they shared a look only family could give each other. Then Hades turned his head to look down at Psyche, completely unphased. "So, I hear you're here for the remedy to Apollo's poison."

"Yes."

"I'm afraid I don't have it."

Psyche blinked, his words not quite registering.

"What he means is that you must be the one to retrieve it," Persephone explained.

"I *was* getting to that," Hades said, then glanced at Psyche. "She really has no sense of humor."

Persephone smiled, please with herself.

Hades stood and Psyche found herself following them through a dark passage once again. They passed rooms full of creatures in strangely superb clothes, holding strangely superb objects. The halls twisted in odd angles and curved and doubled down on themselves, showing sometimes grotesque, sometimes exquisitely beautiful sights, until they finally opened up into a large room with a colossal crack in the middle.

"Is this the entrance to Tartarus?" Psyche asked.

Hades let out an amused sort of snort. "Gods no. You don't suppose I'd keep a door to Tartarus in our home, do you?"

"Yes," Persephone said, "after all, he might fall in and then where would we be?"

He glared at her good-naturedly. Psyche found herself admiring their relationship. They seemed to be truly enjoying each other's company. They seemed to be in love.

"No," Hade explained, "this is Erebus, the darkest point in our realm. Apollo wove his poison from the sun, the light itself, and so you must get the remedy from the darkness itself."

Psyche thought she'd been taking everything in stride, but this was too much. "So, I'm supposed to jump in there?"

"Yes, that is the idea," Hades said.

"But what is it? How do I weave a remedy from it?"

Persephone stepped up to her and put a sympathetic hand on Psyche's arm. "You won't know until you jump."

"Oh," Psyche breathed. Suddenly all of her life choices flashed before her eyes. "A leap of faith?"

"Something like that."

Psyche thought of her family.

Come back, Elara had said.

I will, Psyche had replied, fisting her hands.

Psyche nodded. "I hope you're watching," she said, looking up at Aphrodite. Then she looked down at the crack. It was darker than the night. Than the ocean. Than even the Styx.

She took one small step.

And another.

If she prolonged it for any longer, she'd lose her nerve.

So, with the third step, she jumped.

XXXI Darkness in Light

Eros was in darkness.

He thought he knew eternity. He thought he knew pain. He was wrong.

Then a bright ray of light shone on him.

Darkness cracked.

Eros tried to use it to break free. But a crack wasn't enough.

XXXII Light in Darkness

Psyche fell.

She had never felt this blind before. Nights never got this dark. This was darkness that robbed one of any sense of self. This was... rebirth.

Psyche smiled.

A warm light flickered at the bottom.

She reached for it and caught it on the tip of her fingers.

It floated up and she along with it.

When she was at the top, cold hands pulled her up.

"You did it," Persephone exclaimed.

"She did," Hades repeated, a disbelieving smile on his face.

Psyche looked down and saw that she held a small orb of pure darkness.

"Quickly," Persephone said, rushing her toward the door. "You must hurry."

"Use my personal door," Hades said.

"What other door do you think I was going lead her to?"

He huffed.

They returned to the grand throne room and Persephone indicated to a door behind the dais. Compared to everything else, it looked ordinary.

"I hope we meet again," Persephone said.

Psyche remembered Aphrodite's words about certain death and whatnot, "It might happen sooner than you think."

Persephone opened the door and Psyche stepped through from darkness to a land of grey clouds with veins of crimson pulsing through them.

Cherubs congregated around somebody.

"Eros," Psyche said.

"What are—" the cherubs began to say but they went quiet when they saw the darkness in her hands. Then they parted.

Eros lay on clouds, paler than the moon. His wings, for he had great golden wings, were folded in, and scorched. But he was painfully beautiful.

Psyche approached him. The ball of darkness swallowed all light. And when she neared Eros, it began to draw out light from him.

The cherubs screamed. Because it looked awful.

There was a loud crash as the clouds turned dark and Aphrodite came in with another god, who, judging by his hateful expression, was Ares. Anteros flew in right after them.

Before anyone could say anything, Ares threw a spear at Psyche.

XXXIII The Only Right Thing

Instead of piercing her clean through, the spear was swallowed by the darkness.

"Impossible," Ares said. He tried to throw another one but Aphrodite and Anteros stopped him.

Eros's back arched as the last of the contaminated light was drawn out of him. The ball shrunk and finally disappeared. Eros gasped awake, gaining back his own godly glow.

The relief that coursed through Psyche was hard to describe in words.

"You did it," Anteros said.

Eros looked up at her. "You."

Not the greeting she'd been expecting.

He sat up with a wince. "What are you doing here?"

Aphrodite swept past Psyche. "Having the last conversation of her life."

"She saved you," Anteros said. "Went down to the Abyss of Darkness."

Eros's gaze snapped back to Psyche, so intense and exhausted. "I want to talk to Psyche alone," he said.

"Make it short," Ares said. "Athena is winning the war."

Anteros nodded at Psyche and left along with the cherubs. Ares left next, disappearing in a puff of smoke and blood. Aphrodite fixed Psyche with a begrudging glare and left as well.

Psyche was still puzzling out the meaning of that look when Eros spoke. "So."

She glanced down to where he was sitting on a cloud. "So."

"You went into the darkness for me?"

Psyche inclined her head, suddenly shy. She was talking to Eros himself, after all. Up until this point none of what she did had felt real. It was a dream. It felt like a dream but looking down at him now, with his wings healing and the wisps of clouds lazily floating about, it was all beginning to crash down on her. The weight of what she'd done felt too enormous for her. It was the stuff of heroes, not of little girls. And yet here she was.

Eros took her hand, forcing her to step closer to him. His skin was burning hot as was his gaze. "Now be honest," he said, attempting a light tone, "did you go down there for me or were you simply curious?"

Psyche smiled, her voice tight. "Both."

His eyes bore into her and Psyche felt at a loss. But it made her feel a little better to see him struggling to gain composure too.

"What now?" she asked, entwining her fingers in his.

"Now," he replied, looking at their hands. The clouds began to color the blushing shades of rose and peach. "It depends."

Psyche swallowed. "On whether Aphrodite will kill me or not?"

Eros looked back up at her. "She will not touch you. I promise you that."

"Are you sure?" she asked.

"I thought I wouldn't be able to stand up to her, that's why I kept myself hidden from you and you hidden from the gods. I didn't want her to find out. I didn't want any of them to find out. But I was a coward and I'm not a coward anymore." He stood up, tall and ridiculously well sculpted. "Nobody will harm you."

Psyche believed him. "That's good," she said. "So, you're saying it's safe for me to go home."

"I'm saying it's safe for you to do anything you want."

"Anything?" she asked.

Eros began to nod uncertainly when Psyche reached up on her toes and kissed him. This kiss was slow and sweet. It was two wary souls finding homes in each other.

"I think I love you," she breathed when they stopped for air.

Eros smiled. "I think I love you too," he whispered. Uncertainty cracked his voice as he said, "Will you become my wife?"

Now it was her turn to gape. "Your wife?"

He laughed but not in a confident way. "Yes."

"You'd still want me… I may have taken a swim in the Styx but I am still mortal."

"You what?"

"It's a long story," she started but then thought better of it, since insulting his mother probably would ruin the moment. "The point is, we won't be able to live together, unless you're planning on taking frequent trips to Hades."

Eros tsked, the way a normal human might when their loved ones brought up such morbid topics.

"It's actually not bad there," Psyche said. Visiting hell really did put a perspective on things.

"Psyche," he said, then paused to collect his thoughts. "Psyche." He took her hands. "If you become my wife, I will make you a goddess."

She blinked and blinked again. "What?"

He smiled, softly, as if he'd just picked up a shell from the beach and offered it to her. "So, what will you say?"

Psyche couldn't help the joy that rose up within her. This felt right. This was right. And she said the only thing that was right to say. "Yes."

ACKNOWLEDGMENTS

Thank you so much, dear readers, for reading this retelling of a mythical love story. This novella wouldn't be possible without my family, who have been a huge help in the pursuit of my writing dreams. And of course, it wouldn't be possible without you, the very people for whom I write. So if you enjoyed this book, consider leaving a review on Amazon and let me know if you'd like more retellings from mythology. Thank you!

More Works By Sophia Blis

You can find my other works on Kindle Vella:

It's a Deal
The Mirror of Awakening

Printed in Great Britain
by Amazon